Ghost Elephant

by

W. Bradford Swift

In plundering the planet's treasures, men may
gather riches, but more profound wealth is lost...

Nia Gaines is the newest member of Zak Bate's Eco-Adventure task force—
it's only, she doesn't know it yet. When Nia's parents drag her along on a
business trip to China, the source of their affluence soon becomes clear:
ivory, prized since ancient times for its beauty and never before so rare. In
Beijing's back-alley curio shops, the prices are great...but what's the cost?
The answer will change Nia's world.

Along with Zak Bates, Ra-Kit the Magic Cat and Sampson the Flying Dog,
her journey will shed light on the darkest facets of humankind...but, even
poachers have families to feed, and no solution is simple. What can be done
to promise peace for man and those at his mercy?

FALLING THROUGH THE RABBIT HOLE

Nia Gaines found shopping with her parents to be such a drag, even when they were in one of the most exotic cities of the world. Beijing, China had sounded like such a romantic place to visit, but as far as she could tell, it was simply block after block of old stores filled to overflowing with ancient, and mostly ugly, stuff. Stuff, stuff, stuff. They'd been walking from store to store for hours, which felt like days to Nia. And to think how excited she'd been when her dad, Edwardo Gaines, had invited her to come along on what he'd described as a combination family vacation and business trip.

When does the vacation part start? Nia wondered. So far, she'd been dragged along from one antique store to another, each store with stuff uglier than the last. And the prices on them! Outrageously expensive stuff, as far as Nia could tell, but her father disagreed. The more shops they visited, the more excited he became, which, come to think of it, wasn't all that surprising. He had made his fortune buying old stuff overseas, then returning home to Boston, Massachusetts to sell it for a hefty profit.

So, I shouldn't complain, Nia thought, as they arrived at the next store. Beijing Curio, the sign read. She had a pretty great life thanks to all this stuff, but really, wasn't it time to take a break for food, and after that maybe slip in just a little bit of vacation time? Take in a show or something? She'd learned in school that the Chinese had a long and distinguished history that included several unique forms of dance. How about a dance show? Maybe she could convince her parents that it would be an important part of her education. Nia loved dance in all its many forms. She planned to become a professional dancer. That's all there was to it. Already, she was enrolled for her third year in a prestigious school of the performing arts, and was top in her class both academically and in her dance courses.

"Please, Dad, can't we go get a bite to eat? I'm starving," Nia whined for the third or fourth time.

"I think that's an excellent idea," Alisha Gaines, Nia's mother, piped in.

"Okay," Edwardo finally agreed. "Just this one more shop and we'll break for lunch."

"You promise?" Nia asked.

"I promise. Now, let's see what treasures the Beijing Curio has to offer." Edwardo opened the door for his wife and daughter.

"More dusty, overpriced stuff," Nia muttered, soft enough that her father wouldn't hear. He'd promised food after this, so the last thing she wanted to do was make him mad.

Much to Nia's surprise, she found the inside of the shop clean and well organized, and filled with ornate sculptures that even she could appreciate, many of them made from ivory. "Ivory is the tusks of elephants," she recalled one of her teachers telling her, and tusks were really just the elephants' long teeth on either side of their mouths. Her teacher had gone on to discuss how the elephant populations around the world were endangered because of the high demand for ivory, but Nia had lost interest around that time and couldn't remember the reason for the high demand. Now she knew. In the hands of creative artists, a piece of ivory took on a life of its own and was often transformed into a beautiful work of art.

"Huānyíng, huānyíng," a small man in an embroidered crimson sarong said in a singsong voice. "Welcome, welcome." The shop owner stood only a few inches taller than Nia, who, at fifteen years of age, was an inch or two taller than most of her classmates. She had noticed that most of the Chinese she'd seen were smaller in statute. Noticing his new customers were Americans, he quickly switched to heavily accented English. "Please come in. Welcome to my humble shop," the owner continued, then, noticing Nia behind her parents, his facial expression changed to a frown. "One important rule," he said, staring straight at her. "Look, but don't touch. Understand?"

"Oh, she won't be any trouble," Edwardo said before Nia had a chance to respond, which was probably a good thing. Nia hated to be told what to do by anyone and especially by a stranger who was just barely taller than her.

She watched as her father handed the shop owner his business card, and waited as the frown was replaced with a smile. "Oaaa, please come in. I have many fine things your American friends will enjoy. Low prices as well. I am Chang, your humble servant."

Really? Nia thought. *We'll see how humble and how serving you are.* Nia already didn't like the man. Of course, she didn't like anyone who tried to order her around. She stayed with her parents while Chang showed them around to the various departments, pointing out different items in each area. Then, the tinkle of a small bell above the front door alerted him that a new customer had entered.

"Please excuse me one moment." With a final stern look at Nia, he hurried to the front.

"This is a goldmine," Edwardo said, after Chang had left.

"Some beautiful pieces for sure," Alisha agreed.

"And look at the prices. There's plenty of room for a hefty profit. I think we've hit the motherlode."

As her two parents continued to discuss business, Nia wandered off on her own, already bored by the rows upon rows of antiques. Her stomach growled to remind her how long it had been since breakfast. Suddenly, her attention switched from her hunger pangs to a gorgeous object in front of her. The carving of a line of elephants walking over a crescent bridge seemed to glow from within, the ivory was so brilliantly white. Nia glanced up to the ceiling to see if there was any special lighting showcasing the object, but could find nothing. She moved closer to it, mesmerized by the intricate design, each elephant perfectly carved, connected to the one behind tail-to-trunk with the following elephant slightly smaller.

After a moment more of studying it, she looked around to make sure Chang was nowhere to be seen. She heard his words of warning once again in her mind. *Look, but don't touch.*

I've held fragile objects all my life, she countered, as she picked up the object with both hands to get a better look. As her fingers circled around it, she felt a tingling at the point of contact, and in the next second, she felt herself falling through a black hole of space.

NIBANNA OR BIG TUSKER

Nia awoke lying on her back, but the surface beneath her was not what she expected. Instead of the hardwood floor of the Beijing Curio shop, the ground felt irregular and slightly warm to the touch, though the air felt cool and moist on her face. She sat up and gently shook her head to clear it. As she looked around, a shocked look grew on her face. How could it be? She was no longer in the antique store. In fact, it didn't look like she was even in China any longer.

She stood up slowly and circled around to get her bearings. The coolness on her face came from an early morning mist through which she could make out the ground covered with green bushes and, in the distance, the vague outline of trees. *How in the world did I end up here?* she wondered. *Maybe I passed out and I'm simply dreaming.* But if so, it was the most vivid dream she'd every experienced. She could feel the soft texture of ferns around her legs and hear the distant sound of birds. She took a deep breath and picked up a slightly pungent smell. *Is that animals?*

In the next instant, she felt and heard a deep rumble off to her left where a line of trees blocked her view. She felt a shudder of fear pulse along her spine, but despite it, she felt herself being drawn in that direction almost against her will. She was still several yards from the trees when she heard and felt another rumble, much louder this time. *What's going on here?* she thought. She felt the ground beneath her feet shake, and in the next instant, she had her answer as she heard the unmistakable trumpeting of an elephant. A second later, the trees to one side separated as a huge bull elephant pushed them apart, his head tossing from side to side as he used his massive tusks to free himself from the branches. The elephant had to be the most beautiful and majestic animal she'd ever seen. She remembered watching a show on the Discovery channel with her parents about elephants and knew they were only found in Africa or India. Given the size of this one's ears and body, she must be in Africa.

Nia stood frozen in place by a mixture of fear and wonder. *Get out of its way!* screamed a voice from within. She ran to one side and hid behind a clump of bushes just in time to see several dark skinned men running from the woods. Each carried in his hands a rifle that would have made Rambo proud. Two of the men stopped at the edge of the clearing and took aim at the bull elephant.

Nia knew instantly what was taking place in front of her eyes. *Poachers!* Followed immediately by the realization, *They're going to kill him!* But try as she could, she was unable to move from the spot. She watched in horror as the sound of gunfire sealed the majestic beast's fate. The elephant fell to its knees, then, as if in slow motion, the massive body collapsed to one side where it lay, taking its last few breaths. It tried to lift its head, but the life was already seeping away. With a final bellow of anguish that tore at Nia's heart, the bull elephant died. But the horror continued to unfold before her as men circled around the carcass. In the space of just a few minutes, they had gouged out the tusks from each side of the elephant.

Nia felt like she might throw up, but still she was unable to move. *What's wrong with me? Why don't I do something?* Sure, she was afraid. It was one small girl against five heavily armed and ruthless men, but she felt like such a coward anyway. Surely her dad would intervene in some way.

Then she heard a second voice that she didn't recognize come from within her. *You are witnessing something that has already happened. You are not really where you think you are.*

And with that she felt a shudder pass through her body and the hardwood floor of the Curio Shop beneath her.

"Nia, Nia, my baby. Are you okay?" Her mother's voice penetrated through the fog.

"She's coming to," her father said. "She'll be all right."

She felt his hand beneath her head. She opened her eyes and found him staring down at her, a relieved look on his face.

"What happened?" Nia asked.

"You must have fainted," Edwardo replied.

"We saw you pick up this piece of art, waver a bit, and then you started to fall. Your father was able to catch you just before you hit your head, and I caught the sculpture." Nia glanced over to see her mother with the line of elephants in her hands. "You were very lucky."

"I'll say," Nia agreed.

Her father helped her to a sitting position. "I believe Chang asked you not to touch anything."

"Edwardo, not now," Alisha admonished her husband. "What is important is that she's not hurt and nothing was broken."

"True enough," Edwardo agreed.

"I want it," Nia said, pointing to the object in her mother's hands.

"What?" her two parents asked at the same time.

"I want that sculpture you're holding. I have a birthday coming up next month. It can be my birthday present. Please!"

Nia watched as her two parents stared at each other, a hidden conversation passing between them. Finally, her father nodded. "Well, I guess that's okay if that's really what you want."

"It is. It most definitely is. It's all I'll ask for. I don't even need a party this year."

"Really?" Edwardo said. "Well, then, this might be the best bargain of the day, even with all the other items I'm planning on buying."

Nia stood up slowly and brushed off her jeans.

"Why don't you take it up to Chang and tell him to add it to my bill?"

Alisha started to hand the item to Nia, who quickly backed away. "No, I'd rather you take it to him if you don't mind. I'm still feeling a little unsteady. Maybe you can get him to put it in a box so we can take it with us."

"Okay," her mother replied. "Are you sure you're okay?"

"I'll be fine as soon as I get some food in me. Can we go eat now?"

"Sure, dear. You and I will walk down the street to that small restaurant we saw earlier. We'll let your father finish up his work and then join us." She handed the sculpture to her husband. "Take good care of this and bring it with you when you come."

Edwardo nodded. "Sure thing. I promise I won't be much longer. How about ordering me whatever you're having?"

Nia took one final look at the line of elephants. What magic lay within it?

NIA'S RESEARCH

It took the Gaines family three days to make their way back home to their palatial mansion outside of Boston. They'd moved into the home when Nia was three. It was the only home she remembered, and her room had been redone a number of times to keep up with her age and changing taste. These days the posters of her favorite dancers covered the pale pink walls. The newest addition to the decor sat in the middle of the bookcase that made up her bed's headboard. Nia had instructed Elsa, the maid, to take it out of the box and place it there while Nia watched closely to see if anything happened to her when she touched the ivory sculpture. Nia loved the piece even more where it now sat, but she also had a great deal of respect for its power. She thought about trying to touch it while wearing gloves, but then decided not to risk it. She'd just have Elsa move it around whenever she came in for the weekly cleaning and dusting. *Safety first*, Nia thought.

Despite having over a week of homework to catch up on, Nia couldn't wait to get on the internet to find out more about the poaching problem in Africa. She was aghast by what she found. On one site she read: "Tens of thousands of elephants are being killed every year for their ivory tusks. The ivory is often carved into ornaments and jewelry, with Asia being the single biggest consumer market for such products." She glanced to the sculpture over her bed. Maybe it had been a mistake to ask her father to buy it for her birthday.

On the World Elephant Day site, she was shocked to learn that "Elephant numbers have dropped by 62% over the last decade, and they could be mostly extinct in ten years". *Extinct?* she thought. *No more elephants anywhere on the planet?* The thought was too horrible to imagine, so she read on. "An estimated 100 African elephants are killed each day by poachers seeking ivory, meat and body parts, leaving only 400,000 remaining."

She remembered her vision from the other day. To think that similar nightmarish events occurred as many as a hundred times per day. Nia felt sick. She finally closed her computer and went to bed, but sleep did not come easily that night.

THULA ON THE RUN

Nandi could feel the anxiousness of the elephant herd behind her, wanting her to pick up the pace as they drew closer to the watering hole. They had spent an extra day grazing and everyone was thirsty. But they had her baby Thula to think about. *Let them practice a little patience,* she thought, as she glanced behind her to make sure Thula was keeping up.

At just over three hundred pounds, two-month-old Thula's development was right on track. Though her consuming over ten quarts of milk every day placed a strain on Nandi's body, that was a part of motherhood. That and constantly worrying about the little one.

No one is thirstier than me, Nandi thought. She found herself drawn forward by the smell of fresh water, so much so that she almost missed the second smell coming from the same direction. And then it was so strong that she wondered how she could have missed it before. She stopped suddenly and felt Thula bump into her back leg. The rest of the herd stopped as well, though clearly not happy with her for doing so.

All except Thula's father, Lugard, and his impetuous brother. They'd been out of sorts all day and now chose to ignore Nandi's signal of warning. Did they not smell the humans? Human smell without any humans in sight was never a good sign. She would speak to them once this incident was...

Her thought was interrupted by the sharp crack of a rifle, followed a second later by a burst of gunfire. She waved her trunk in the air, trumpeting a warning, but the herd had already turned as one, scattering in all directions, away from the once inviting waterhole that had suddenly become a deathtrap.

Nandi turned and pushed Thula toward a crop of trees about forty yards away. A second round of gunshots sent a chill coursing through her body as she half expected to feel the pain of being wounded, but evidently the shots were not directed toward her. She pushed her baby forward with her trunk into the relative safety of the trees. Panting from a mixture of fear and sudden exertion, Nandi looked around to find three of Thula's aunts hiding in the trees as well, also breathing heavily and exuding an odor of fear. Nandi felt Thula shivering against her leg, still small enough to hide under her.

Nandi pushed a tree limb to one side in order to view the watering hole. Her breath caught in her throat at the sight of the two bull elephants lying on their sides like twin grey mountains of flesh, their blood mingling with the creek water that fed the pond. Both were surrounded by dark-skinned men. She had seen enough. It wasn't the first time she'd witnessed such a brutal attack. She knew what was to follow. She still had nightmares about her first time watching the removal of the tusks. She turned around to signal for the other elephants to exit through the back of the trees. *My Thula will be spared such a sight for as long as possible,* Nandi vowed. They would need to find another source of water somewhere else, and soon.

NIA'S DREAM

Nia went to bed with the atrocities she'd learned about still on her mind. To help her fall asleep, she finally resorted to repeating, over and over, the mantra she'd learned from her meditation teacher.

As she finally drifted off, she found herself in a strange and beautiful land that reminded her of the wide open vistas of Africa she'd seen in the Discovery channel documentary. Only here, animals of every description strolled around with no apparent concern about being attacked by the other animals. Gazelles and zebras grazed on the succulent grasses while a pride of lions looked on in apparent disinterest. All was calm and peaceful, and Nia found herself feeling just as serene, despite being within a few dozen yards of the lions. She watched as a pack of jackals trotted by.

She heard and felt a deep rumbling behind her. She turned to find an elephant lumbering slowly towards her, his massive ears flapping in the breeze. "I know you," Nia said, as he approached within a few yards and stopped. For such a large elephant, she was surprised that it didn't have any tusks, then she realized why. They'd been left back on Earth. "I saw you murdered by poachers."

"Yes, that was me," the elephant said in a deep rumbling voice that Nia heard as well as felt. "I'm Nibanna, and I am sorry to have to expose you to such a brutal sight, but I felt it important that you know this is what is happening in Africa even now."

"Is that where I am now, back in Africa?" Nia asked.

"No, this is the Spiritual Frontier where animals come when they have finished their time on Earth. That ivory over your bed was once part of one of my tusks. I believe it is what made this connection possible."

Nia nodded. She had figured the same thing.

"I called you here because I need your help," Nibanna continued. "My family back on Earth is in grave danger. My daughter, Nandi, has recently given birth to her first baby. Her name is Thula. She is very special, as are all babies, but in Thula's case, she is destined to be a great leader of her kind if she can survive. Lugard, her father, was recently killed by poachers while defending his mate and baby. They are in hiding in Africa somewhere on the Thula Thula Game Reserve lands."

"But what can I do?" Nia asks. "I don't know the first thing about Africa."

"I know," Nibanna replied. "It is unfortunate, but that is the way it is. The Cosmos operates in strange ways at times. It has thrown us together.

You are my only hope. You must save my family." As Nibanna spoke, he began to fade.

A moment later, Nia awoke. She glanced up to find the ivory sculpture over her bed glowing. The light slowly diminished.

I wish I had never touched the darn thing, Nia thought. *That's what I get for not doing as I'm told.*

After trying to go back to sleep for half an hour without success, Nia finally turned on the light and pulled out her tablet. She started searching for an organization or animal rights group that she might pass Nibanna's problem on to, but none of the ones she came across felt right, until she read an article about a young boy and his dog who had created such a commotion at the World Summit on Global Warming in Rio de Janeiro, Brazil. She then did a Google search on his name, Zak Bates, and found his blog, where he regularly wrote about the challenges the animals of Earth faced. He also had a section of fantasy stories about a young boy joining forces with a magic cat and a giant flying dog to rescue animals around the world.

Boy, what a vivid imagination, Nia thought, as she finished reading one of the tales. Still, according to several online articles, he had actually given the speech in Brazil and had swayed the leaders to reconsider their position when it came to several environmental issues affecting animals. Maybe he would know who to talk to in order to help Nibanna's family.

She next surfed over to Facebook, where she found Zak Bates' personal page. She requested to become one of his friends, then messaged him as well. Before finally retiring to bed for a couple more hours of sleep, she texted her Uncle Maynard, a Boston police detective, to see if he could use his skills to get Zak's phone number. Uncle Maynard always said that Nia was his favorite niece. Time to find out if that was true.

FACEBOOK FRIENDS

Zak reached over to place his iPhone's alarm on snooze for the third time, then remembered he had set it to go off earlier than usual so he could finish the blog post he'd started the previous night. He pushed himself up in bed and switched off the alarm, glancing at his notifications as he did so, noting he had a Facebook friend request. He clicked on it and waited for the Facebook app to open, discovering he had a friend request and message request from the same person, Nia Gaines. *I don't know anyone by that name,* Zak thought, as he clicked over to her Facebook page just to be sure. *She's pretty,* he thought as her profile picture came onto the screen. It must be some mistake. While she appeared to be about his own age, he felt certain he would remember her if she were from his school. He noticed all the pretty girls, even though he didn't have the nerve to speak to any of them. That is, except for Allie, who was pretty enough, in a tomboy sort of way. But this Nia Gaines was anything but a tomboy. She was breathtaking, with her light chocolate complexion and long, curly dark hair that formed a halo around her face. He scrolled down the page to where there were several pictures of her dancing, along with a video that appeared to be her at some kind of dance recital. *Man, she's good,* he thought as the video played. *Pretty and talented. No question, her friend request and message must be a mistake.* He decided to check out what the message said anyway.

I need your help!

What a strange message, Zak thought, growing more suspicious. Maybe this is one of those scams his parents kept warning him about. Maybe Nia Gaines is really a three hundred pound man whose real name could be found on the pedophile list, and this was his way of preying on young kids. But if so, he'd sure gone a long way to pull off the false identity with detailed photos and videos. Zak continued to scroll down, growing more confident that Nia Gaines was a real person and not some scam artist, but that still begged the question: *What does she want with me? Well, why not click the friend confirm button and find out?* He was just about to do that when he heard a sound of "plink, plink" against the window. *What was that?*

He heard another series of them -- "plink, plink, PLUNK!" That last one sounded like it might have cracked the window pane. Zak climbed out of bed and walked over to the window. Staring out, he saw this two companions, Ra-Kit and Sampson staring up at him from the ground below. Ra-Kit, who claimed to be the last remaining magic cat, sat on her haunches and appeared to be in deep meditation while Sampson, the giant Newfoundland dog who was her traveling companion, stood beside her. Zak was still staring down at them when the next barrage of pebbles struck the window. Where had they come from? Neither Ra-Kit nor Sampson had appeared to move, then Zak realized that must have been why Ra-Kit seemed to be meditating. *She must be using her mind to toss the pebbles at the window.* Zak waved his hand, gesturing for her to stop before she woke the rest of the family. Sampson nodded at him, then raised one paw to his ear in the universal motion of someone talking on the phone. Zak nodded back and returned to pick up his phone from the bed where he'd left it. Upon activating it, he noticed he had a text message, but without a name or number. He clicked over to it.

Urgent meeting of the Eco-adventure Team, the message read.

Eco-adventure team? He had to admit, he kinda liked the sound of that.

Call Allie. Meet in the park before school.

Wait a minute, Zak thought. *Neither of his four-legged teammates owned a cellphone, so how could he be receiving a text message from them? Were Ra-Kit's magical powers growing stronger?*

Before he could ponder that line of questioning further, the phone rang, making Zak jump. *Whoa, this is starting out to be a busy day filled with surprises.* Not recognizing the phone number, he clicked the button to screen the call. A moment later, the message came across the screen, "This is Nia Gaines, Zak. I need your help! Please pick up."

It's her, the girl from Facebook! What do I do? Should I take the call? What would I say? Despite having finally made friends with a girl, Allie, he was still far from comfortable talking with a girl he didn't know, especially not a beautiful one, and especially when it felt a little like she was suddenly stalking him. *Don't be ridiculous. She's hardly the type of girl that would be stalking someone like me.* But the question remained.

What should he do? Before he could do anything, the call disconnected and a second later he heard his mom, Calida, calling him to breakfast. *Wow, what a morning.* He quickly threw on a pair of jeans and a blue and white striped t-shirt. The blog post would have to wait. He texted Allie about the emergency meeting before going down for breakfast.

RICH KID ONLY CHILD

The next morning, Nia sat at the kitchen table engrossed in her cellphone, as she munched on French toast and sipped on her second cup of cappuccino, when Alisha strolled in. "What's the rule about cellphones at the kitchen table?"

"I tried to tell her," Mandy, the cook, said from across the room. "She just ignored me. Would you like a glass of orange juice with your coffee this morning, Ms. Gaines?"

"Yes, please, Mandy. Thank you." Nia's mom turned from the cook to her daughter. "Well?"

"Mom, did you know that there are tens of thousands of elephants killed every year by poachers and that the markup on the black market for ivory is a thousand percent, which means that the poachers themselves make very little money from the animals they kill?"

"Please, do we have to talk about such matters so early in the morning?" Alisha replied as she sat down across from Nia. "You're as bad as your father. Morning should be a pleasant time to connect with our loved ones, not try to solve all the world's problems. Now, put away your phone and finish your breakfast."

Nia tried unsuccessfully not to huff and roll her eyes, but then did what her mother asked.

"Why the sudden interest in elephants?" Alisha asked, as she took a slice of toast from the bread basket and started buttering it.

Nia paused before answering. She considered telling her mom about the strange vision she'd had in the antique store and her dream, but then remembered her tendency to freak out about anything out of the ordinary, which would invariably lead her to make another appointment with her shrink. In this case, she'd probably book an appointment for both of them.

"Oh, it's just for a school assignment," Nia replied instead.

"That's nice. I'm glad you're taking an interest in something other than dancing," Alisha said.

"Mom, that's not fair. Must I remind you I've made the honor roll for the last two semesters?"

"Well, you know what they say: 'Of those to whom much is given, much is expected', or something like that," Alisha said, then quickly changed the subject. "Remember, your father and I will be leaving in a few minutes for another one of his business trips. Your father has ordered a car for us so that Jacob can take you to school and pick you up afterwards. Please don't hang around in the hall chatting with your friends. He gets nervous when you do that." She leaned over and gave Nia a kiss on the cheek. "Remember, do what Jacob and Mandy tell you and don't give them any backtalk."

Nia nodded, but her thoughts were already elsewhere, working out the details of her own trip. One that would likely result in her being grounded for life.

ECO-TEAM MEETING

Zak hurriedly wolfed down his raisin bran cereal and rushed out of the house to meet Ra-Kit and Sampson. As he crossed the street to the regular meeting place in the park, he noticed Allie arriving as well on her bike, and nodded to her.

"Thanks for making it on such short notice," he said as she pulled up beside him and climbed off her bike.

"Sure thing," Allie replied, "but what's all the hurry about anyway?"

Zak shook his head. "I don't really know. I just woke up a short time ago as Ra-Kit was about to break my window throwing stones with her mind."

"She can do that?"

"Evidently. I'm not sure, but I think either her magical powers are growing or she's becoming much more creative in how to use them. I even received a text message from her somehow."

Allie shook her head in amazement. "She's a constant surprise. There they are," Allie said, pointing across the park. "Who's that with them?"

Zak looked in the direction she pointed. "Why, I think that's…yes, it's Grace the Gazelle. She's from the Spiritual Frontier I was telling you about the other day."

"She's gorgeous," Allie replied. "I love her shade of lavender."

Zak leaned over close to his friend. "Sampson says he thinks it's from a bottle, but I agree. She's beautiful. I wonder what she's doing here?" *And how was it even possible for someone from the Spiritual Frontier to be here on Earth?* he wondered.

The two of them waved to their fellow Eco-Team members as they approached. Ra-Kit sat on her haunches cleaning herself until everyone was together. She briefly introduced Grace to Allie before sharing the reason for her being there.

"As you may recall, Zak, Grace is the leader of the Herbivores, and she's quite concerned about one particular family. Grace, would you like to explain?"

"Sure," Grace replied, stepping forward. "Nibbana is one of our most honored residents of the Spiritual Frontier. He was a great tusker elephant when he lived on Earth and is still an important part of our community. He's been extremely distraught about what is happening here on Earth with his fellow elephants. Thousands of them are being killed each year, many of them by poachers, who cut away their tusks to be sold on the black market. Recently, one of his own family members was killed by poachers, as was Nibbana himself many years ago. He is particularly concerned for his great-granddaughter, Thula. She and her mother are currently in hiding after Thula's father was murdered."

"Why, that's terrible!" Zak exclaimed.

Allie nodded. "I'll say? What can we do to help?"

Grace glanced over at Ra-Kit and Sampson. "They are just as wonderful as you said. I'm so grateful you are willing to help. This will be a dangerous mission. Probably the most dangerous one you've been on to date. These poachers don't mess around. They have been known to shoot and kill any humans who get in their way."

"They don't scare me!" Zak replied angrily, then smiled sheepishly. "Well, that's not exactly true. They do scare me just a bit, but what I meant to say is that I won't let that fear stop me from doing what is right."

Allie nodded her agreement.

"And that is the mark of true courage," Grace replied. She turned to Ra-Kit. "I seem to be fading."

Ra-Kit nodded. "I'm afraid so. It's taking a lot of effort to keep your image here, but that's okay. I'll fill them in on the rest. Thanks for letting us know about this. We'll do our best to help Thula and her family. I understand that she has a special destiny."

"That's correct," Grace agreed. Zak noticed that she was indeed starting to become transparent. He could just make out the park through her. "She's to become a great leader like her grandfather, that is, if the poachers don't get to her first."

"But she's just a baby," Allie said. "Surely, she's not of any value to them, at least not yet."

But already Grace had grown so faint that it didn't appear she'd heard Allie's comment.

"You're right," Ra-Kit spoke up. "She has no value to the poachers for ivory, but she's a very special elephant. The native tribes in the area refer to one of her kind as a "Ghost Elephant". You see, Thula is all white from the tip of her trunk to the end of her tail. Such elephants are very valuable, even as a baby. She's in incredible danger, make no mistake. That's why we'll be leaving for Africa in the morning. Pack your bags."

"What about me?" Allie asked. "Am I to remain here again as central command?"

"No, not this time. You'll be coming with us, at least as far as the animal reserve where Thula lives with her family. We'll set up our communication headquarters there."

Allie spun around in a dance of excitement. "Super! We're off to Africa!"

"But how are we all going to get there?" Zak asked, glancing at Sampson with a concerned look on his face.

"I've had a breakthrough in warping," Ra-kit replied. "More specifically, a breakthrough in helping Sampson to warp. We will all be virtually weightless for most of the journey once we get into the warp stream. There's really nothing to worry about. Trust me."

But even though Zak did trust Ra-Kit with most things, her ability to keep Sampson steady while in the warp stream was not one of them.

"This should be exciting," Zak muttered under his breath, but loud enough that Allie heard him.

"You can say that again!" Allie exclaimed with far more enthusiasm than Zak felt.

THULA IN HIDING

Nandi looked over at baby Thula, lying on her side asleep. *At least one of us can get some rest,* she thought. They'd walked several miles away from the watering hole to where they found shelter in a growth of Acacia trees. The aunts had spread out in search of another source of water, leaving the two of them to recover from the morning ordeal.

After a few minutes, Thula stretched her legs as she awoke, before standing up. *I'm hungry,* she communicated to Nandi, who walked over so she could nurse.

If I don't get food and water soon, there won't be enough milk for my baby, Nandi thought. *Please find water soon.*

Where are the others? Thula asked, after she'd finished eating.

Out looking for water, Nandi replied.

Will they come back?

When they find water, they will let us know, and we'll go to them, Nandi replied.

How about father and Unc? Will they help?

Nandi paused, uncertain how to answer. Finally, she decided the truth was best. *No, they will not. They've already done their part.*

What do you mean?

They distracted the men and gave us time to escape.

But where are they? Thula persisted.

They are on their way to a new land, one without poachers.

I want to go there. Can we go there now?

Someday, but not today, Nandi replied, stroking her baby with her trunk. *I pray not today. Now, rest. We must conserve our energy. We may have a long trek ahead of us.*

A couple hours later, Nandi felt the deep rumble she'd been waiting for. The aunts had found something and were summoning her to join them, but it felt so far away. Would they be able to travel that far? There was only one way to find out. She nudged Thula awake.

Come, my precious, it's time to go.

VILLAGE LIFE

A small village outside Ntambanana, South Africa

Musa Abara watched his mother sweep the dirt floor for what had to be the thousandth time and wondered once again why she bothered. After all, it was dirt to begin with and would be dirt when she finished.

"Let me do that, Mamma. Father will be home soon and you know how angry he gets if his meal isn't ready."

Thabiso looked up from her task and smiled at her son. "That would be most helpful. It won't take long to fix his food, though. Warmed up from yesterday's meal. Just pray he doesn't notice."

"He's been longer than normal with his friends. I doubt he's in any condition to notice much of anything," Musa assured her. He took the broom from his mother and danced around the room with it. A combination of his diet and love for dancing had resulted in a slender, yet wiry, build. His dance instructor once compared him to Fred Astaire, but had then added, "Astaire with two left feet," and then laughed. Musa had joined in, knowing there was a compliment in her words somewhere. A few days later, he viewed a YouTube video of the famous dancer and realized what a generous comment it had been.

A few minutes later, as Musa put the handmade broom away in the corner of their one room hut, he heard a commotion outside like someone stumbling, then a second later, the door flew open and his father staggered in, caught his balance at the last second and roared, "I'm home and hungry. You have my food ready, woman?"

"Hush up, old man," Thabiso countered, pointing to the table where she'd placed a covered dish just moments before. "You're not at the pub now, so you don't have to shout."

"True, true enough," Zunga replied in an only slightly softer voice. He stared bleary-eyed at his wife. "My men and I will be going out on a hunt again in a few days. That'll mean fresh meat for our village and treasures to trade if we are so fortunate." He turned his attention to Musa, who sat on his haunches trying to go unnoticed. "You ready to join us? It will be a good hunt."

"No, he's not ready," Thabiso spoke up, before Musa could respond. "You promised me, no hunt until he's fifteen and that's still a few months away."

"Oh, woman. Let the boy speak for himself," Zunga roared again. "What do you say? It's time you put away the trappings of a child and became a man."

Musa remained sitting, staring back at his father. Finally, he shook his head. "I have school and dance afterwards," he mumbled.

"Ugh! What a waste of time," Zunga countered, as he wobbled over to the table and sat down. He lifted the cover from his food and dug into it like a ravenous dog. He'd eaten over half of it before looking up. "Same poor excuse for a stew as yesterday," he observed. "I work hard all day and this is all I get for it? This and a bunch of lip from my son? What is this world coming to anyway? Bring me that bottle in the cupboard over there."

Thabiso returned to the table with a cup of water instead and placed it next to his plate. "You finished off the bottle two days ago, need I remind you. Besides, you've had more than enough to drink already." She took a step away before continuing. "Our son's education is not a waste of time, nor is his dancing. He is smart and gifted."

She turned to Musa. "You will remain in school and enjoy your dancing. You will be a man soon enough. Now, go fetch me some firewood so I can be prepared to cook the bounty your father is promising to bring home."

Musa nodded, thankful for any excuse to get out of the house for a few minutes. He had to hand it to his mother. She was a small woman by stature, but a brave and passionate one, especially when it came to her son. *Like a mother tiger,* he thought. He knew a large part of her courage came from her being a sangoma, a practitioner of traditional African medicine, which had earned her a special position in the village. One that came with responsibility, but also respect. She was well known for her ability to heal physical, emotional and spiritual illnesses. Musa suspected it was these special gifts that made Zunga just a little nervous around his wife. It helped to keep a tenuous peace most of the time.

MAKING IT UP

"Miss Nia, we need to leave now or you'll be late for school," Jacob called up to her from the bottom of the spiral staircase, his chauffeur hat in one hand and a key fob in the other.

Nia came down the stairs, pulling a lavender suitcase on wheels behind her. "Sorry, Jaco," Nia said, using the nickname she'd given him when he'd first come to work shortly after she'd turned four. There's been a change of plans. I just received a text message from Mom." She waved her cellphone in the air. "They want me to join them on their business trip after all. Says it'll be educational. I say, 'boring.'" She rolled her eyes for emphasis.

"But, they just left less than thirty minutes ago, and they didn't say anything to me about it," Jacob replied, a frown growing on his face. "Maybe I should…"

"Well, you know my mom -- Miss Spontaneous, if ever there was one," Nia said, as she pushed the suitcase in his direction. "She's already called an Uber for me, so there's no changing her mind. At least, that lets you and Mandy off the hook for babysitting me while they're away." She stood on her tiptoes and gave him a peck on the cheek. She really hated deceiving him this way, but at least he could claim he knew nothing about her plans when her parents found out about them later.

Since he had been part of the family for most of her life, she'd learned he was best handled by being kept off balance, as he was now. She knew how he felt. She hadn't fully planned all of this out herself, but she recalled her father often saying, "Sometimes you have to make it up as you go." Then, he'd wave his arms in the air to take in his surroundings, the palatial home with the acres of rolling hills and manicured gardens. "There are times you just have to be willing to take a risk and make it up as you go. That's what I did that led to all this."

27

So, I'm just taking dear ol' Dad's sage advice. Certainly, he can't fault me for that.

This much she had planned. After being reminded that her parents would be out of town for several days, she had hurriedly packed her own bag and grabbed her passport. She also still had one of her father's AMEX cards that he'd failed to reclaim from their previous trip, along with a few hundred dollars in cash she'd squirreled away from her weekly allowance. While eating breakfast, the harebrained idea had started bubbling to the surface, right after she'd verified that there was indeed a Thula Thula Private Game Reserve in South Africa. She then reserved a ticket for Richard's Bay, the closest airport to Thula Thula.

"Oh, there's the car now. Gotta run! Be a jewel and tell Mandy goodbye for me, will you?"

"Ahh, well, I guess. I mean, this is all quite irregular. Maybe I should…" Jacob stammered, clearly unsure what to do about the sudden change.

"No time. You know how these Uber drivers hate to be kept waiting," Nia replied as she rushed out the door to the navy blue SUV she'd summoned from her phone ten minutes earlier. She waved to him one last time, then motioned for the driver to stay where he was. She opened the rear door and threw her suitcase in while the driver looked on in amazement. Nia paused for an instant. "What's your name and what's my name?"

"Why, I'm Pete," the driver replied. He glanced down at the computer screen next to him. "And I'm here to pick up Nia Gaines, so I'm assuming that would be you, correct?"

"Correctamundo," Nia said, as she joined her luggage in the back seat. "Onward to Logan, please. My flight leaves out of Terminal E."

As the SUV made its way through the early morning Boston traffic, Nia took the next step in her plan. She opened her suitcase and brought out a set of hair extensions and her makeup bag. She figured she had at least forty-five minutes to transform herself from a teenager into a young woman of the world. It shouldn't be that hard. She planned to sculpt her new identity to look as much as possible like the pictures she'd seen of her mother when she'd been in her twenties, and she had her mother's mannerisms down already. Her main goal was to get on the flight to Richard's Bay by way of Heathrow and Tambo International Airport without anyone questioning why someone her age would be flying by herself for the almost twenty-four hour trip.

She was off to save baby Thula, even though she didn't have a clue how she was going to do it.

NIBANNA & GRACE

"You know I can't do that," Grace said, smiling at her old friend, Nibanna.

"But you have to let me return to Earth," the great tusker replied. "My family is in great danger, especially Thula. My family's entire legacy could be wiped out. Surely, just this once…"

"You don't understand," Grace interrupted him. "It's not just that I'm not permitted to honor your request, I'm physically unable to do it."

Nibanna stared at her for several seconds as he continued to look for a way around her reply.

"But, you returned just recently."

"No, I didn't. I just sent my image to Earth and that took Ra-Kit's magic to pull it off even for a short time. I don't think that's what you're asking, is it?"

A forlorn Nibanna slowly shook his head. "No, I need to be there, not just some illusion that could disappear at any moment. I guess it's all up to Nia," he mumbled this last under his breath.

"What was that?" Grace asked.

"Oh, nothing."

"No, really. What did you say? Who or what is a Nia?" Grace asked, a look of concern on her face.

Nibanna didn't say anything. *I may have put my foot in my mouth…again. When will I ever learn?*

"Well?"

"She's a young girl that…well, we connected. I can't really explain how, though I think it had something to do with a piece of one of my tusks she touched." He went on to relay what had happened.

"So, she's going to help you in some way?" Grace asked.

30

"I don't know. I think so. I hope so," Nibanna replied. "Not sure what one little girl can do, but it's the only hope I have at this point." He rocked from side to side in an effort to dispel his growing apprehension.

Grace stepped forward and nuzzled his trunk. "Oh, friend, that may not be your only hope. I have been in touch with Ra-Kit and Sampson. They are on the way to Africa with their young human friends. Try not to worry. They will represent us well, and do everything in their power to save your family."

Nibanna looked up. "Ra-Kit is going to Africa?" A look of hope appeared on his face for the first time.

"As we speak," Grace replied. "Now, about Nia."

"Yes?"

"You know that we're not supposed to interfere with matters on Earth, right?"

"Yeah, I know," Nibanna replied. "It wasn't my intention. It just happened. Like I said, I don't even know how."

"Well, please be careful. The rule is quite clear. We're not to interfere with anything that happens down there." She paused. "But sometimes we do."

WARP TIME

Zak and Allie met Ra-Kit and Sampson in the field behind Allie's mother's veterinary clinic early the next morning before the sun had even risen. They all knew the earlier they left, the less likely they would be detected. For once, Ra-Kit's prediction that everything would go smoothly turned out to be accurate, even with the added payload of Allie that Sampson had to carry. Zak found it to be the smoothest warp trip he'd experienced so far. Maybe Ra-Kit's powers had grown since their last mission, or maybe Allie was his good luck charm.

As they came out of the warp zone, he immediately felt the difference in the air temperature and humidity. Even considering that they were a few hundred feet above the ground, the air passing by them felt much cooler than he'd expected . He leaned over to take a look below, being sure to keep a good grip on Sampson's fur. Sure enough, beneath them he could see the rolling savannah, with a herd of zebras galloping across it.

"What time is it anyway?" Zak asked, as Sampson slowly descended in a wide circle, preparing to land.

"If my calculations are correct," *Which they almost never are coming out of a warp,* Zak thought, "...it should be close to noontime."

"Really? I thought Africa would be warmer than this."

"Well, I might be off my time estimate," Ra-Kit continued, "but remember, South Africa is in the southern hemisphere, so we're actually in their winter period."

"Oh, yeah," Zak said. "I didn't think about that." *So, maybe I should have brought a jacket or sweater,* he thought, as he shivered from the cool air rushing by. He glanced down again.

"Where's this Thula Thula Game Reserve you were telling us about?"

Ra-Kit nodded to her left. "Over that way a few miles. I didn't want to run the risk of being seen."

Zak groaned. He started to ask if Sampson could fly them a little closer, but already knew the answer, so didn't bother.

He turned his head around as far as he could to glance at Allie, who had her arms securely wrapped around his waist since they'd taken off.

"Everything okay back there?" he asked. "You're awfully quiet."

"I'll be okay. Just a little motion sickness," Allie replied in a weak voice. "I'll feel better once we're on the ground."

"That makes two of us," Sampson replied. Zak remembered how strange it was that the only flying dog he'd ever met was actually afraid of flying, but did it anyway because of his commitment to their missions.

Soon, the four of them were all on the ground after Sampson made a perfect four paw landing. Zak and Allie climbed off of his back and they both stretched, then laughed at copying each other.

"That was exciting!" Allie exclaimed, "Even if it did make my stomach turn cartwheels. And to think, we're already in Africa. That's truly amazing. Where to now?"

"That way," Ra-Kit said, pointing straight ahead from where she sat on Sampson's shoulders.

"How far will we have to walk?" Zak asked, as they started off in that direction.

"I'm not completely sure," Ra-Kit replied. "From the position of the sun it's clearly later than noontime, so my calculations appear to have been a bit off the mark."

"As in wrong," Sampson added.

"So, we don't know how far it is to the reserve, do we?" Zak asked, trying hard not to groan. He was all too familiar with some of the consequences of Ra-Kit's imprecise calculations.

"Not exactly," Ra-Kit admitted. "But I'm positive it's in that direction. Probably just over that ridge there. Onward, Sampson. The Eco-adventure Team to the rescue!"

Zak figured at least an hour had passed when he began to notice the grassland they'd been walking through changing, with an increase of low lying shrubs and bushes, none of which he recognized. *Perfect places for hungry animals to lie in wait,* he thought, and less than a minute later, he felt the hairs on his arms stand to attention. What was that large lump over there beneath that tree? *OMG, it's a lion.* Before he could alert the others, he spied another similar object, and then another and another. He stopped in his tracks, but Sampson, who was walking in front of him leading the way with Ra-Kit on his back, continued on. Allie bumped into him.

"Hey, what's up?" Allie blurted, "Where are you brake lights?"

Zak pointed in the direction of the pride of lions, who hadn't seemed to notice them yet. At least he prayed that was the case. "Sampson, stop!" Zak whispered, but with an intensity that surprised him. "Lions!"

Sampson took another step or two before turning around at that last remark. "What? Where?"

"Over there, under those trees," Zak replied, continuing to point in that direction. "And it looks like they've seen us," he groaned. Suddenly, an "eco-adventure" to the wilds of Africa didn't seem like such a good idea. He watched as a large male lion slowly stretched before standing up. The three female lions lying closest to him also stood up.

"Holy crap! We're in trouble now," Zak said, still whispering, but loud enough for everyone on the team to hear.

"You can say that again," Allie added.

Zak reached behind him with one hand without taking his eyes off the lions, who were growing more active by the second, in an effort to assure her that everything would be all right even though he didn't believe it himself.

"They're coming this way, and there are more of them in the bushes." Sure enough, Zak counted at least ten more tawny colored shapes beginning to move, each one materializing into a lion.

"Wouldn't be surprised if there's not twice that number," Sampson added, in a voice that sounded surprisingly unaffected by their situation. "A pride of lions can often number over thirty."

"Oh, great. Thanks for that little factoid," Zak said. "What do we do?"

"Well, what we don't do is panic," Ra-Kit spoke up for the first time. "Just stay calm."

"Easy for you to say. You're riding on top of a flying dog. How about Allie and me?"

"Trust me," Ra-Kit replied.

Zak groaned. *Famous last words,* he thought. How many times had he trusted someone, just to regret it later. But Ra-Kit wasn't just anyone. She was the last living magic cat. He had learned to trust her in several other dangerous situations, and so far, it had all worked out well. That's why he'd accepted her invitation to go on this trip. He'd known it was going to be dangerous, but they were a team, and teammates had to learn to trust each other.

"Okay," Zak finally replied. "Lead the way." And, much to his surprise, Sampson and Ra-Kit did exactly that. Sampson resumed walking. *Wait, I didn't mean...* but then he smiled, and shrugged, and resumed walking as well. A second later, he felt Allie grab his hand and walk beside him into a pride of lions.

AIRPORT TROUBLES

Logan International wasn't the largest airport Nia had been to, but it was one of the busiest, even mid-morning after the first schedule of flights in and out. But at least she felt fairly comfortable there, having accompanied her parents on various trips through the years, as well as meeting them upon their return. She checked the board and saw that her flight to Heathrow had been delayed, so decided she had time for a quick snack before heading to her gate. She found a restaurant with only a few people inside. Everyone seemed more intent on scurrying to their new destination than eating, which at least meant she'd get served quickly.

She immediately experienced a difference from her new, sophisticated look, with the waitress coming over promptly with a pot of coffee. Nia turned the mug right size up indicating she did want coffee and then ordered a bagel with cream cheese, her mother's favorite snack. *May as well play the part full out,* she thought, as she gazed around at the few other travelers.

The waitress had just returned with her food when a young man, dressed in a custom-fitted suit and pulling a black carry-on behind him, strolled in and looked around. Seeing Nia, he smiled and walked over.

"Good morning," he said, with an air of confidence. "I'm Mark. Do you mind if I join you. I hate eating alone, though it's often a part of my job."

"Yes, I understand completely," Nia replied in an effort to match his air of success. "Flying from country to country can be such a hassle, especially these days with all the security issues."

"Exactly," Mark replied, sitting down. He waved for the waitress and held up the empty mug, indicating he, too, wanted coffee. After the waitress left, he pulled his cellphone out of this jacket pocket and glanced at the time.

"My flight was delayed for at least four hours. Can you believe it?"

"Unfortunately, yes, I can," Nia replied, with a flip of her hair. "Mine has been delayed as well."

The two ate quietly for a few minutes, until Mark leaned over to her. "You seem to be a woman of the world. I have an idea. Why don't you and I go to the hotel I'm staying at. It's only a few minutes away by shuttle. We'll relax, have some fun. Maybe take a dip in the pool, you know." He gave her a knowing wink.

Nia stared at him, shocked by the invitation but trying not to show it. *How would mother handle such a situation when she was in her twenties,* she wondered. *It doesn't matter,* she decided, *because I'm not in my twenties. I'm still a teenager.*

"No, thanks," she replied. "My flight isn't delayed that long."

He leaned in closer. "I'll make it worth your while." He tapped his breast pocket.

Are you kidding me? Nia thought. Her eyes flitted around her. The few other travelers that had been sitting in this section had already left. Should she call for the waitress? What should she do? A plan started to form in her mind. She took a quick inventory of what she'd packed that morning in her bright pink carry-on case. Not really that much and nothing that couldn't be easily replaced once she arrived in London. She decided to teach this jerk a lesson.

"Give me a moment. I need to freshen up. Would you keep an eye on my bag?"

"Sure thing," Mark replied. "Give my invitation some thought. I promise you a good time."

Nia smiled demurely. "Oh, I'm sure," she replied, as she rose from the table. "I'll be back in just a minute and give you my answer."

She sashayed in the direction of the bathroom, glancing back at the last second before going through the door to see that Mark had pulled his phone back out and was texting someone.

She took a right hand turn out of the restaurant. As she passed the checkout counter she pulled a twenty dollar bill out of her pocket and tossed it on the counter. She still had her I.D., passport, money and her father's AMEX card. She rushed down the hall towards her gate. Seeing a couple of security guards standing together talking, she slowed her pace.

"There may be a completely legit reason for this, but I just noticed something kind of suspicious," she said, smiling at the larger guard.

"What's that, ma'am?"

"There's a man who just came into the restaurant where I was sitting carrying two bags. One was bright pink. He seemed quite nervous."

The security guard nodded. "Might just be his wife's or something, but we'll check it out. Can't be too careful these days."

"Thank you, officer," Nia replied. "That's what I thought, too."

She turned to leave. She wished she could be a fly on the restaurant wall listening in as ol' Mark tried to explain himself to the officers.

MUSA TRIALS

Most days, Musa didn't mind the forty-five minute walk to Tnambanana, but today he was in a hurry to get to the dance studio so he could try out the new steps he'd come up with during the night. At least with the cooler weather, he wouldn't arrive hot and sweaty, and he didn't mind finishing his allotted time with his instructor that way. As he entered the outskirts of the only town within thirty miles of his village home, he felt a quickening of his pulse. He always enjoyed the energy he felt from the larger town even though it was still relatively small by most people's standards.

He watched as other people mingled about, some carrying baskets of fresh produce, others herding their goats or sheep to market. He watched as several women carried on their heads large pottery pots filled with water. He was tempted to swing by the market, but knew that would make him late for his appointment, something he'd done only once before and vowed never to do again. Jailin had told him flat out that she didn't have any use for students who couldn't be on time, and if Musa wanted to continue to study dance under her, he better never be late again. He never had, and he vowed not to be today.

As he rounded the corner, he heard the distant chiming of the town clock marking the quarter hour. Fifteen minutes to spare. He much preferred coming early rather than slipping in at the last minute. He'd done that once before and Jailin had then spent ten minutes relating the story about ancient ships that occasionally sailed too close to the rocks, only to have a change in the wind or tide propel them onto them. "So, you can choose to sail close to the rocks if you like, Musa. Just beware of unexpected winds or tides that could make you late." Another lesson learned and not needing to be repeated.

He entered the brightly painted door with the silhouette of a dancer emblazoned across it. It really felt like his second home, and in some ways he often felt more loved and cared for here than he did at his true home, especially when his father was around and had been drinking. Time to show Jailin his new dance steps and spend the next hour sweating while doing something he loved.

"Hey, Zunga, isn't that your boy over there?" Kacho, one of Zunga's long time friends and a member of his poaching gang, asked.

"What are you talking about? Musa is home doing his chores." *At least he better be,* Zunga thought, then looked over to where his friend was pointing. "Well, son-of-a…That is him. What in the world is he doing here?" But even as he asked the question, he looked above the door that Musa was just now entering and knew the answer: Jailin's Dance Studio.

"What? Is your boy studying to be a ballerina or something?" Kacho said with a chuckle, and several of the other men heading to the bar laughed with him. "Maybe he'll be a great success and make enough money dancing to take care of you and your woman in your old age."

"Not likely," Zunga replied, none too pleased to be laughed at by his friends.

"Why not?" Kacho continued. "You never know."

"Yes, I do know," Zunga barked back. "I know because I'm putting a stop to this nonsense this very minute. Go on to the bar. I'll meet you there after my son and I have had a little chat."

He waited for his crew to move on down the road and in the meantime, tried to calm down a little, but he was still simmering with anger when he opened the door to the studio, where he found Musa sitting outside in the waiting area.

"Why aren't you home doing your chores?" Zunga asked, with a growl in his voice.

Musa shot up in his chair at the sound of his father's voice. "How did you know I was here?"

"One of my men had to point it out to me. Damn embarrassing that I don't even know where my son is. Now, get on home where you belong. We'll deal with the rest of it later."

Musa sat there without moving. He stared down at his hands resting in his lap for several seconds before replying. "I'll go home and finish my chores before I go to bed tonight. I promise I will, but I'm staying for my lesson."

"You talking back to me?" Zunga asked, his voice now barely above a whisper, but it still carried an edge of authority that cut through the space between them. "I told you to get yourself home…NOW!" He shouted the last word so it reverberated throughout the studio and into the next room, where Jailin was finishing up with another student.

"No, sir," Musa replied. "Mamma already paid for the lesson, and it wouldn't be right for me not to stay."

"So your mother is in on this, is she?" The volume of Zunga's voice continued to rise. "I should have known it. Well, I won't have you wasting your time and her hard earned money on such a silly…"

"What is going on out here?" Jailin said, as she entered the room. She was a tall, stately black woman who wore her hair in dreadlocks with beads woven throughout it. "And who are you?" she asked, staring at Zunga with a mixture of curiosity and contempt. "More importantly, why are you disrupting my class?"

Zunga, momentarily taken aback by the woman's beauty and imposing manner, stepped back, then pointed at Musa. "I'm his father, and he's…he's…" He stopped to try to get his senses about him, then began again. "I don't want him wasting his time when he should be home doing chores."

Jailin glared at Zunga for several seconds before finally replying. "Fine. You're his parent, so take him home. Talk it over with your wife. Let me know what you decide." She turned to Musa. "Go on home now with your father. I won't charge you for today's lesson. Let me know what you work out."

"But, I don't want…" Musa started to say, but stopped when he saw a frown forming on his teacher's face. "Oh, all right," he finished instead. "But I'll be back. I promise."

"You shouldn't be making promises you can't keep," Zunga said, waving his son to the door. "Now, get yourself home. I'm already late for my meeting."

"Yeah, right, meeting," Musa muttered as he started walking slowly to the door, his shoulders hunched in resignation. "Meeting over a few pitchers of beer, no doubt."

Zunga swung at him, but Musa deftly danced under the blow and out the door, leaving his father behind with Jailin.

"Your son is really quite talented," Jailin said. "He's one of the best students I've ever had. I do hope you allow him to continue with me."

"Sure, sure," Zunga replied. "Just keep looking up in the sky."

"What?" Jailin asked.

"For the pigs flying. That's when you'll know I've given my permission for him to return."

PRIDEFUL LIONS

Don't look them in the eye. Whatever you do, don't stare at them, Zak thought, remembering what he'd read about how to deal with an aggressive dog or other animal. Would it work on lions? He prayed it would.

He repeated the instruction to Allie, who continued to clutch his hand, which felt strangely good despite the situation they were in.

"It's a little hard not to," Allie whispered back, "knowing at any second I might become their dinner, but I'm doing my best."

Zak nodded and tried to swallow, but he found his mouth was as dry as the Sahara desert at the other end of Africa. *Never let them see you sweat,* his dad and brother often liked to say in such situations, but then again, when had they walked through a pride of lions? This was entirely different from going out for Little League or the first time he had asked a girl to dance. He'd sweated plenty in those instances as well.

Now they were completely surrounded by the pride. Lions to the right, to the left, and straight ahead, but the worst were the lions he couldn't see, but could hear and feel behind them. *Just waiting to pounce of my skinny little body,* he thought, then berated himself for it. Thinking such thoughts would not help him stay calm and present to what was going on around him. He had to be brave for Allie if nothing else. He'd been the one to get her in this fix after all.

The two teenagers continued to walk a few feet behind Sampson, who kept a slow pace so they'd have no problem keeping up with him. He held his head high and looked straight ahead, so Zak decided to do the same. *After all, we've been in worse situations than this,* though, at the moment, he couldn't think of any nearly this dangerous.

He estimated they were probably about half way through the outcropping of trees that the lions called home when one of the male lions, the one that appeared to be the oldest, and was definitely the largest lion Zak had ever seen, lifted his head to the sky and let out a mighty roar.

Oh boy, here goes! Zak thought, just before he stumbled and came to a halt at the same time Sampson also stopped.

Then, a strange thing happened, perhaps the strangest thing Zak could remember ever seeing on Earth. Oh, sure, they'd seen plenty of unusual sights when Ra-Kit and he had visited the Spiritual Frontier, but nothing like this had he ever seen here on his mother planet.

The giant, tawny-coated lion, with a mane that any animal would have been proud to wear, knelt down in front of them, and one by one, each of the lions around them did the same.

"It's Ra-Kit," Allie whispered reverently, for surely this was a holy moment. "They're paying homage to her."

"You're right," Zak replied. "To the last living magic cat." He felt the tears well up in his eyes and a knot grow in his throat. Suddenly, he remembered why he loved animals so much: for their dignity, their magnificence, their beauty. *This is why I'm here. This is why I'm part of the Eco-adventure Team.*

Time seemed to stand still; Zak wasn't sure how long it lasted. Finally, Ra-Kit, still on Sampson's shoulders, stood up and nodded to the alpha male. The king of beasts rose from his bow, then he and the rest of his pride disappeared into the surrounding foliage. Zak Bates and the rest of the Eco-adventure Team resumed their trek to Thula Thula. Zak sniffled and, a second later, he heard Allie doing the same thing.

TEAM ARRIVAL / TOKABO

It was late in the afternoon when two tired teenagers walked into the Thula Thula Game Reserve with a giant black dog leading the way and a scruffy black cat walking beside it. The main building of the reserve had been visible on the horizon for the past hour, but only now, as they entered through the gate, did Zak take a moment to study it. It appeared to be an ancient palace from some bygone era with massive walls that towered thirty feet in the air and columns on the second floor highlighting two large windows. Despite its obvious age, someone had taken great care to restore it to its former glory.

"It's beautiful," Allie said, standing next to him with a look of awe on her face.

"I'll say, but what in the world is such a magnificent structure doing out here in the middle of nowhere?" Zak asked.

"An eccentric millionaire from England purchased close to a thousand acres of land in the late 1800s for his private hunting grounds," Ra-Kit answered. "He loved ancient Mayan architecture, so he had the building constructed as a replica to use as his lodge. He left it to his daughter, who converted it to what it is today."

"No wonder it looks so out of place," Allie said.

"Out of place and out of time," Zak agreed.

They resumed walking, thankful that their long journey on foot was finally over. Several people who saw the motley crew approaching paid them little attention, being too busy taking care of their own tasks. However, as they approached the steps leading up to the mansion, a large black man came down to block their way.

"Well, what do we have here?" he asked, in heavily accented English. "Look what the dog dragged in…literally." He chuckled at his own joke. "Where in the world have you come from? Certainly, not from out there?

Though, to look at you, I'd say you've had a long trek getting here. It's a wonder you weren't eaten alive."

Zak stared at the man for several seconds, trying to figure out what to say that would sound reasonable and at the same time not be too large a lie. He came up with nothing. His brain felt frozen, locked in standby mode. He glanced over to Allie, who looked as stunned as he did. *I guess I should have thought this through more clearly sometime over the last few hours.* He glanced at Sampson and Ra-Kit, who both sat obediently next to each other like two well behaved pets. They weren't going to be any help.

"Where are your parents?" the black man asked, clearly directing the question to Zak.

Back in North Carolina, Zak started to say, but knew that would simply create more confusion, so instead, he just stood there looking down at his dust covered shoes.

"Come now," the man continued in a softer tone. "I'm just trying to find out where they are so I can get you back to them. Of course, I'll have to talk to them about the no pet policy we have here as well, but that shouldn't worry you none. Listen, my name is Tokabo. What's your name?"

Finally, a question he could answer. "Zak. Zak Bates, and this is Allie." He pointed to the two animals. "And that's Sampson and Ra-Kit."

"Okay, good. Now we're getting somewhere," Tokabo replied, smiling. "I bet you all are hungry, yes?"

Zak and Allie both nodded. "And thirsty," Allie added.

"I bet you are. Ol' Tokabo will be happy to get you something to eat and drink...," he paused for just an instant, "...just as soon as you tell me where your parents are."

Zak groaned silently. He eyes scanned across his team once again, hoping against hope that someone would step up and answer the question, but clearly it was left up to him. "Well, you see...let me try to..." Nothing. He simply had nothing that was going to sound plausible enough to get them inside and to the promised food and water.

"Well, they've finally arrived!" The loud, booming voice came from behind Zak. "Tokabo, I see you've met my friends."

Zak turned around to see a tall, lanky man with long blonde hair approaching them as he dusted off his pants.

"Sure thing, boss. Just trying to find out where their parents are so I can..."

"Oh, don't bother with that now. I'll take over from here." He turned to Zak and Allie and spread his arms in greeting. "Welcome to Thula Thula." His eyes flitted over to Sampson and Ra-Kit. Had that been a look of recognition? This man apparently expected them, but how was that possible? Zak stared at Ra-Kit for a long moment, but the black cat just sat there licking one paw and then cleaning herself with it.

"Go on about your duties. I'll make sure our guests are well taken care of," the man continued. Tokabo nodded and walked away, shaking his head.

"Whatever you say, boss."

After he left, the man turned to Zak and Allie. "I'm David Shedrick. It's a pleasure to meet you, Zak and Allie."

"You know who we are?" Zak asked, bewildered by the sudden turn of events.

"Of course I do," David replied. He turned to the two animals. "And it's good to see you two again as well."

"Now, wait just a minute," Zak blurted out, suddenly angry. He stepped toward Ra-Kit. "You knew we'd be expected and yet you said nothing this whole time?"

Ra-Kit stood up and yawned. "Well, it would hardly have been appropriate for me to speak up. David here is the only one who knows who I am and why we are here. Besides, I wanted to see how you handled the situation. I must say, you need practice dancing with unexpected occurrences, but that will come in time, I'm sure."

"Oh, so that little episode was just part of my training. Is that what you're telling me?"

"Well, that's certainly one interpretation," Ra-Kit replied. "But really, now is not the time. We have work to do." She turned her attention from Zak and back to the man. "Good to see you again, David. I trust all is well with you and your family?"

"Yes, we're fine, but I'm afraid I can't say the same for the animals. You've arrived at a most opportune time. We're having a devil of a situation with poachers recently."

"Well, how about getting us some of that food and refreshment your assistant was trying to blackmail us with, and telling us all about it?"

"Happy to do so," David replied. "Please join me in the house. Bhava, as our African friends call it." As they all started towards the bhava, he continued, "So, Tokabo tried a little blackmail on you, the master of blackmail?"

Ra-Kit nodded. "Well, he tried it on Zak, and it might have worked if you'd not come along when you did."

So, David knew Ra-Kit well enough to know that she wasn't above using blackmail to get her way, Zak thought as he joined them. His mind drifted back to the first time he'd met the magic cat and how she'd used his love for Angus, his Cairn terrier, to persuade him to join her cause. *Just how well do these two know each other?* The question quickly disappeared as he walked into the dining hall and found before him a spread of food that would have put most all-you-can-eat restaurants to shame.

Tokabo walked around to the back of the mess hall and pulled out his cellphone. He didn't know who the kids were that suddenly showed up unannounced, and with their two pets to boot, but he knew someone who'd want to know about them. He punched in the number. After a few rings, he heard someone pick up.

"Yeah?" was all the man said by way of greeting. *A man of few words,* Tokabo thought, once again irritated by having to speak with him.

"We've had a development here that I thought you'd want to know about," Tokabo said, then waited for a reply. Several seconds went by.

"Well?" the man asked, clearly irritated he'd had to use a second word needlessly.

"A couple kids showed up with a large black dog and a scruffy cat." Another pause.

"So?" The irritation grew.

"Well, you told me to call you if anything out of the ordinary happened here, and this is certainly not normal. Shedrick acted like he knew them and was expecting them, but he's always told me about guests arriving in the past. This seems fishy to me."

"Got it," the man replied. *Wow, two whole words,* Tokabo thought, then decided to change the subject.

"How's my sister?" There was an even longer pause on the other end of the line.

Finally, "She's fine. Do your job, and she'll stay fine." The line went dead.

Tokabo stared at the phone for a second before waving his arms in frustration. That man. What in the world did his sister see in that jerk? *Do your job!* He was doing his job, but the more he did it, the more distasteful it was becoming. *Time to get back to my other job,* he decided. *My real job. The one I get paid for here.* He stomped away to resume his chores.

Zak stood up to refresh his drink. As he walked by the side window he gazed outside. It was still hard to believe he was in Africa, despite having trekked over what seemed like half of it in the past few hours. But there it was in all its glory, and there also was that strange man with all the unanswerable questions talking on his cellphone. *I wonder who he's harassing now?* As he watched, the man threw up his hands. Maybe not. *Maybe someone's bugging him for a change.* Zak shrugged. *Couldn't happen to a nicer guy,* he thought, as he finished filling his glass with iced tea and returned to his table where Allie and David were still chatting away.

RICHARD BAY

Nia couldn't figure out why her parents enjoyed traveling so much. While she enjoyed discovering new and often exotic places and meeting interesting people, the actual process of getting from point A to B was usually a hassle at best, and all too often a downright nightmare. Thank goodness her layover in Heathrow gave her enough time to take a cab into London. She found it so freeing not having to deal with a bag that she decided not to replace the one she'd left in Boston. *I'll just pick up a toothbrush and a few other items when I get to my final destination*, she thought.

All she really needed at this point were the proper clothes for the short stay in South Africa. She found some in a small cheque store next to the tourist center. "This is what everyone who's anyone is wearing for safari these days," the clerk had insisted. Nia decided she liked how she looked in the khaki short-sleeved outfit, complete with padded shoulders and a wide belt that accentuated her youthful figure nicely, except for the hat that came with it. It looked more like a helmet than anything. In fact, the clerk referred to it as a Pith helmet. "Made from authentic Scholapith," the clerk continued. Nia started to ask what in the world Scholapith was, but then decided she really didn't care. She had doubts about the silk scarf that wrapped around the helmet and trailed behind her, but the lady insisted it pulled the entire outfit together with simple elegance.

The Richard Bay Airport bustled with travelers from around the world. As Nia stepped off the Dash-8 turboprop airplane and onto the tarmac, she looked around. It seemed to Nia that it didn't matter how remote an airport was or how small, there were always crowds of people rushing around frantically trying to make their flight, and often becoming frustrated when they finally reached the gate only to find that their flight had been postponed or even cancelled.

She strolled through the airport with an appearance of quiet calm she didn't feel. During the flight she had realized what a leap of faith she'd performed heading off to a foreign country with little or no plan. Now she was in a city she'd never even heard of before booking the flight, in a location where she knew absolutely no one. What was she thinking when she'd started out on this insane mission to save a baby elephant that she didn't actually know was even real? It could have all been made up by an overly active imagination -- a dream brought on by a mixture of too rich a meal coupled with a tired body.

But no, she shouldn't second guess herself. It had been much more than a dream. It had been two different episodes and both had felt so real, like she'd actually been in Africa watching the brutal murder of a beautiful animal, and later meeting him in the Spiritual Frontier. She just needed to trust herself more. As she had the thought, she straightened her shoulders and smiled. Confidence. That was the key. *Never let them see you sweat,* her father had often told her, particularly just before an important dance recital or other situation where sweating seemed inevitable. Like finding yourself in a strange foreign country without any real plan for what to do next.

You put one foot in front of the other, she again recalled hearing her father say. *You make it up as you go.* Well, she could do that. After all, she was his daughter with his blood and DNA coursing through her along with that of her mother, who was far from a wilting wallflower. Both her parents were successful adults, and it was time to show them what she was made of as well.

She strolled through the concourse feigning confidence, using the way her mother walked as a model. She followed the signs to baggage claim, not that she had any baggage to pick up. She had just the one bag that she'd taken with her on the plane, but she knew this was where she'd find transportation to her final destination. At least she hoped she would.

As she walked along, she listened to the voices around her, many of which were in English but with a definite accent, but also others of a wide range of languages that she did not recognize, much less understand. Just one more item she'd not taken into account. Would there be a significant language barrier where she was headed or would everyone speak English? She thought she remembered reading somewhere that South Africa's primary language was English, the area having been settled in the late 1800s by the British. Still, it would be a good idea to find a local guide, someone who knew this area better than she did, which would be practically anyone.

If she thought the baggage claim area was frenetically busy, it was nothing compared to the outside area where a mixture of mostly aged cars and trucks blended with various other modes of less modern transportation including bicycles and rickshaws. And people, people everywhere in a wide array of garb, though Nia noticed that none were wearing the latest African safari outfit except her. Had she made a mistake shopping in London rather than waiting to see what people actually wore in Richard Bay? Too late now. She glanced around, looking for a sign, something like "Dependable Local Guides Here," but of course, there was no such sign. No, she'd have to find a guide on her own, but before she figured out how to go about that, the challenge resolved itself.

"Oh, Miss, you really need my help, and I am at your service."

Nia looked around for the source of the comment, but didn't see anyone that seemed to go with the voice. Then, she looked down to see a young boy, probably not more than ten or twelve, glancing up at her with a wrinkled hat in his hands.

"I am Sherlock, Miss, and I'd be honored to be your guide, please, Ma'am. You need my help, no?"

"Well, I don't know," Nia replied. "I was really thinking of someone a might bit…"

"No, Ma'am, I'm your boy," Sherlock interrupted. "I know the area, having been born here, and I am honest." He waved around him to take in the crowd. "You can't count on everyone being honest."

"Really? Then how can I count on you being honest? Wouldn't a dishonest person claim to be honest?"

"True enough," Sherlock replied with a smile. "But would a dishonest person tell you the truth, that you are a sitting duck for being taken advantage of, given how you are dressed, or would they simply take advantage of you?"

Nia stopped to consider the point and decided it had merit. She'd begun to think she'd made a mistake in her choice of clothes. "So, what would an honest person do about that?"

"We will start by getting you clothes that won't have you stand out as an easy mark," Sherlock replied, then reached down at his feet and pulled up two handfuls of dirt from the curb, and threw them on Nia, who gasped and jumped away too late.

"That will help just a bit in the meantime." He studied her for another few moments, then removed the floppy hat from his head and handed it to her. "Put this on."

Nia removed the Pith helmet and handed it to him before donning his. He studied her again. "Better. It'll have to do for now. Please, come this way. I will help you stay safe and get you where you need to go. By the way, where is that?"

Nia smiled. She liked this young boy and felt she could trust him, so she replied, "Thula Thula. Do you know it?"

"Oh, yes, Ma'am, I know it well. It's not too far away. Very nice area. They do good work to help our animal friends. I'll get you there safely, but it's too late in the day to drive there now. I know a place you can stay the night. Nothing fancy, but mostly clean and safe. In the morning, I'll get you some clothes and we'll head out. Yes?"

"Yes," Nia replied and stuck out her hand. "I'm Nia Gaines and you have a new customer. Lead on."

MOUNTING CRISIS

"What's thaaa sumph?" Zak asked, with a mouth full of one of the most delectable sandwiches he'd ever eaten.

"Didn't your mother ever teach you not to talk with your mouth full?" Allie asked. "Now, take a second…Wait, what's that sound?"

"Exactly my question," Zak replied, after taking a long swallow of water. The sound of rushing air grew.

"Oh, that's our sky copter," David replied. "That's Dr. Dondi returning from her latest trip to care for some of our sick or injured animals."

"Dr. Dondi?" Allie asked. "I think I read something about her on the internet."

"Probably so," David continued. "Her name is actually Donna Diora, but everyone around here just calls her Dr. Dondi. She's become quite an internet sensation since a couple YouTube videos went viral. She's quite embarrassed by the whole thing, but, as I pointed out to her, those videos have helped our fundraising efforts tremendously."

A couple minutes later, Zak saw the helicopter come into view across the field and when it landed, a young woman wearing green flight pants and a matching blouse climbed out and jogged towards them, her brown hair swirling around her face from the wash of the copter's rotating blades. As she entered the dining hall, David introduced the two teenagers to her, but simply introduced Ra-Kit and Sampson as their pets.

Donna smiled at everyone, and took a minute to offer her hand for Sampson to smell before patting him on his broad head. "What a handsome boy you are!" she said, as she continued to pet him. It struck Zak odd to hear someone talk to the giant dog as though he were only a pet and not part of a team of incredibly talented animals and humans. "So, it's a pleasure to see a dog and cat getting along so well with each other," she said, turning her attention next to Ra-Kit, who sat on her haunches, apparently above it all.

"Oh, yeah, they're best friends," Allie pointed out, smiling knowingly at Zak.

"How was your outing?" David asked, as Donna walked over to fix herself a sandwich and grab a bottle of water.

"Pretty routine," Donna replied. "A few bumps and bruises, a zebra that had a nasty gash on her side. Nothing too serious, thank God, after the days we had last week."

"What happened last week?" Zak asked.

Seeing that Donna had just taken a big bite of her sandwich, David answered for her. "We had two different attacks from poachers. The first one wasn't too serious. We got there in time before any animals were harmed, but the second group was better armed and trained. We lost two elephants from that one."

"It's the toughest part of this job," Donna added, after taking a drink from her water bottle. "Getting to the scene after the fact, and knowing there's nothing you can do. It's heartbreaking."

"I bet," Allie replied. "My mom is a vet back in the States, and losing one of her patients is hard for her as well. How long have you been a sky vet?"

Donna counted on her fingers. "This will be my fourth year. I worked in the U.K. for a couple years after graduation, but then this opportunity arose, so I jumped on it. Been some of the best years of my life and some of the hardest." She shrugged. "But I wouldn't change a thing."

Zak looked over to Allie and whispered, "Sounds like we've arrived just in time."

Allie nodded. "Sure does. But what are we going to do...?"

Before she could finish the sentence, they heard a series of rapid fire gunshots, followed by a few seconds of silence, then another series of shots.

"What in the world?" David shouted, as he jumped from his chair.

"Sounds like they're back," Donna replied, dropping the sandwich on the plate in front of her and wiping the mayonnaise from her lips.

"Maybe we can catch them with the copter," David said, as he started towards the door.

"Won't work," Donna said. "We were almost out of gas when we got back. It'll take too long to refuel. We'll need to use the Jeep."

"Not large enough," David countered. "We'll take the Land Rover."

"What?!" Donna exclaimed, as she stopped to stare at her boss. "You can't be thinking about bringing them along. It's too dangerous."

David shook his head, "They're all coming. I'll explain later. Go find Tokabo and have him bring three rifles and ammo. Meet me at the Rover ASAP." Donna hesitated for only a second before nodding and rushing out the door.

"She's right, you know," David said, after she'd left. "These poachers are dangerous hombres. They won't hesitate to shoot anyone or anything that gets in their way. Are you sure you're up for this?"

Zak and Allie stared at each other before nodding. "Yep, it's what we do. Ra-Kit will keep us safe, won't you?" Zak replied.

"Well, even my magic isn't all that effective against speeding bullets," Ra-Kit replied. "But I'll do everything I can to be sure it doesn't come to that if I can help it."

"Okay, let's go." David started towards the door. "Tokabo has had quite a bit of experience dealing with poachers through the years. It's one of the reasons I hired him. Whatever he tells you to do, don't question it. If we do run into them, things could get bad fast."

Zak nodded. What had he gotten himself and his best friends into this time? Wait a minute. Hadn't it been Ra-Kit who'd gotten him into this fix? *Hardly matters at this point*, he thought. *We're all in it now up to our necks.* Even with the rush of adrenalin, his knees felt weak.

A BLOODY MESS

It took close to thirty minutes before they finally found the remains of the poachers' attack near a watering hole a couple miles from the reserve's compound. Among the outcropping of savannah trees lay the carcasses of two dead bull elephants. Not only had they been shot several times, but their tusks had been removed. The blood of the two elephants soaked into the ground. Zak felt his stomach lurch as he fought back the urge to lose his recently eaten lunch. He glanced over to Allie to see that she looked a bit green as well. *What have we gotten ourselves into this time?* he wondered again. This was far more serious than he'd ever suspected back home.

"We're too late," Allie said, finally breaking the silence.

"Yes, we're too late for these two," Ra-Kit replied, glancing over to make sure Donna wasn't within range to hear him. "But not for the rest of the herd."

"But where are they?" Zak asked, turning to David, who had a look of disgust and anger on his face.

"No telling," David replied. "Though it looks like they took off in that direction." He pointed in the direction of the setting sun. He turned to Donna as she approached. "Make sure the helicopter is refueled and ready to go first thing in the morning. We need to find the herd and do whatever we can to protect them until these brutal murderers are apprehended."

Donna nodded, but remained silent. *Are those tears I see?* Zak wondered. Of course, these weren't merely beautiful animals that had been brutally slaughtered. They were part of Donna's family that she'd devoted the last four years of her life caring for, only to see them end up as bloody bodies lying on the ground.

"Is this the same herd that Thula and the rest of Nibanna's family are a part of?" Allie asked.

"Yes, it is," David replied, "but how do you know about Thula?" He glanced over to where Sampson and Ra-Kit stood. "Never mind. Stupid question. What else do you know about Thula?"

"Only that she's destined to be a great elephant and leader of the herd," Zak replied.

David nodded. "Yes, I've suspected as much. Once you see her, you'll understand why, but that will have to wait for another time. There's nothing else we can do here. Let's head back."

As they all started back to the Land Rover, Zak held back for a final look at the devastation, which was probably the only reason he noticed Tokabo gazing off into the distance. He'd not said a word the whole time they'd been there. What had David said about him? That he'd had previous experience with poachers? Suddenly, Zak felt a shudder run along his back. What had that look been on Tokabo's face? Had it been one of relief and satisfaction?

ZEBRA MANE

The Zebra Mane Bar had served as his father's hangout for as long as Musa could remember. Musa found it to be a dark and dirty building that smelled of unwashed men and stale beer where his father's lowly friends met to talk about the disgusting things they did to stay alive.

"I thought that bull elephant had me for sure," Mondo, Zunga's right hand man, said before taking a gulp from his beer.

"Yeah, you should have seen your eyes. Looked like two full moons," Zunga added.

"He appeared out of nowhere," Mondo countered. "I've never seen such a large animal just suddenly materialize from thin air."

"Hell, I saw him barreling down on you when he was still fifty yards away," Zunga laughed. "But you weren't paying attention. Too caught up taking out the other bull, I guess."

"Well, all I know is that it was a great hunt," another of Zunga's men said. "Maybe one of our best yet."

"And most profitable," Zunga added. "Those tusks will bring in enough money to keep our village fed for at least a month." His men nodded. "To the hunt!" Zunga shouted, lifting his beer glass in a toast. The six men all clinked glasses before emptying them. "Hey, Yano, another round over here. Can't you see we're thirsty? We have much to celebrate tonight."

A rotund black man wearing a stained apron wrapped around his belly waved back. "I'm coming, I'm coming. You're not my only customers, you know."

"Maybe not, but you'll find no more loyal clientele than us," Zunga countered, then wiped his mouth. "Hey, boy, sit up and pay attention." He slapped Musa on the shoulder. Musa did what he was told. He'd learned long ago not to disobey his father, at least not when the old man had been drinking. Zunga turned his attention back to his men. "My son will be joining us soon. It's time we had another great hunter in the family."

The men cheered and raised their empty glasses in a mock toast.

"In fact, I'm planning a hunt to end all hunts to celebrate the occasion." The men cheered again.

"Tell us more," Mondo said.

Zunga shook his head. "Not yet. Still a few details to work out. I will say that it'll make today's escapade look like a stroll by the lake in comparison. Hey, Yano, show Musa those pictures you took today, especially the one where Mondo is about to get trampled by that bull before I saved his life."

Yano nodded and pulled from his back pocket a cellphone that had seen better days. He flicked it on and found the pictures before walking over to where Musa sat. "Maybe after this next great hunt, we'll be able to buy a new cellphone. This one is just about shot." He handed the phone to Musa, who thought about refusing to take it until he glanced at his father, who simply nodded to him.

"See what you have to look forward to," his father said. "Go on." There was a note of edginess to those last two words.

Musa did as he was told, taking the offered phone. He glanced down to the first photo and gasped. For an old phone, it took surprisingly vivid pictures. The first photo was a closeup of a bull elephant's head minus the tusks that had been dug out of their sockets. A pool of dark red blood stained the ground below it. Musa felt sick to his stomach as a wave of nausea and disgust passed over him. How could someone brutally kill such a magnificent beast and then, on top of it all, brag about being a great hunter? Musa had seen the rifle that his father used. He'd watched his father spend over an hour dismantling it for cleaning. It was a sophisticated semi-automatic killing machine. Great hunter indeed!

"Go on, look at the rest of them," his father ordered.

As Musa flipped through photo after photo, the nausea mounted. Coupled with the sickening smell of rank beer and sweat, he knew if he didn't get out of there, he'd only add to the disgusting odor with his own vomit. As he rose from the table, he handed the cellphone back to its owner.

"Where do you think you're going?" Zunga asked.

"I need some air," Musa said, ashamed to hear it come out as a whine.

"Sit down!" Zunga ordered, but this time Musa didn't obey. Instead, he just stood staring at his father. Finally, the dam burst.

"How could you do that?" he asked, pointing at the phone. "How could you murder such a beautiful creature of God, and then claim to be some great hunter? Grandpapa would be ashamed of you."

Zunga rose from the table and towered over his son. "That old man was nothing but a weak and heartless drunkard who was stuck in the past. His stupid old traditions."

It takes one to know one, Musa thought, but knew better than to say so. "Grandfather was an honorable man who respected the earth and all its inhabitants."

"Are you talking back to me?" Zunga said, slurring his words. "You just wait a few more months and see what it's like out there. We have our own traditions to honor, including the oldest of them all. It's survival of the fittest. Just wait, you'll see," he repeated.

But Musa had heard more than enough. He whirled on his father. "I'd rather die than join your band of bloodthirsty murderers." He started for the door.

Zunga lunged at him, but he was too drunk and Musa was too quick. Musa easily sidestepped away and ran out.

A deathly silence followed. Every eye was on Zunga, who stood weaving in the center of the room. Finally, he chuckled. "The boy has spirit, you gotta hand it to him." He turned back to the barkeep. "Where's that round of beer?" He staggered back to his seat and was about to sit down when his cellphone rang. He pulled it out of his pocket to answer it.

He listened for several seconds and a smile began to form. "That sounds just fine. Keep me informed," Zunga said to whomever was on the other end, then disconnected the call. "Make it two rounds on me. It's going to be a very good hunt."

NO STAR HOTEL

Nia followed Sherlock deeper into the city until they arrived at a tall, rundown building desperately in need of paint and repair.

"What is this?" Nia asked.

"It's where you will stay tonight," Sherlock replied. "I promise to return in the morning. No worries."

"Stay here? Is it even open? It looks like it's been deserted for years. How many stars does this hotel have?"

Sherlock laughed. "City-girl is funny." He paused, then, noticing the look on her face, added, "Oh, sorry. You're not kidding. Do not worry about its rating. It is safe and the rooms are relatively clean. That's all you need to know about it."

Relatively? Nia thought. *What's that supposed to mean?* But she decided she was too tired to worry about it now.

"Sleep well. I will return in the morning." And with that, Sherlock turned and ran away.

"Wait!" Nia shouted after him, but it was too late. He'd already disappeared around the corner. The last thing she saw of him was the Pith helmet bobbing through the crowd.

She glanced up at the building where she was to spend the night, and chuckled. Across from the faded sign, someone had scrawled the words:

No Star Hotel

I wonder if Sherlock had a hand in that? Nia thought, as she let out a deep sigh and entered the hotel.

Inside, the lobby area wasn't as bad as she had feared. Everything was old, and it felt like she'd stepped back in time to the fifties or sixties, but like Sherlock had said, it was clean. She checked into a room on the third floor, remembering that her father had told her to always request staying on that floor. "It's high enough up that you aren't likely to have burglars try to enter through the outside, but low enough to get out if there's a fire." The thought of burglars and fires didn't give her a warm feeling of security just now, but the logic made sense to her.

She dropped down on the double bed, which creaked under her weight, and was almost instantly asleep, only to find herself once more in the Spiritual Frontier with a very troubled Nibanna standing before her.

"What's wrong? Is it Thula?" Nia asked. She stepped forward and reached out to stroke the giant elephant's trunk.

"No," Nibanna replied, "at least not yet as far as I can tell. But two others of my family were killed earlier today. It's just a matter of time before they get Thula and the rest of the herd. I'm afraid they will all be joining me here before their time."

"I'm sorry to hear about your loss," Nia replied, continuing to stroke his trunk. "I'm almost there. I'll be at the reserve in the morning."

Nia felt Nibanna's mood lift, but only for a moment. "I'm thankful for what you are trying to do," Nibanna said, "but I don't see how you will be able to stop a gang of killers."

Me either, Nia thought. *What in the world was I thinking? It seemed so much simpler back at home. Get on a plane, fly to Africa, save a baby elephant, and fly home a heroine.* But now it was time to face reality. She was a young girl completely out of her element, in a foreign country where violence and killing were a way of life for many.

"I don't know what I'll be able to do," Nia confessed, but then added, "but you mustn't lose hope. I need you to be strong so that I can be strong. We're in this together, right?"

Nibanna nodded. Nia leaned in and placed her head against Nibanna's trunk. They stood there for several seconds, comforting each other until Nia felt Nibanna's head becoming softer. She awoke to find herself back in her bed in the hotel pushing her head into the pillow. It was dark outside. How long had she been sleeping? She sat up and looked around, still groggy from her nap. She pulled out her cellphone that had reset to the local time upon her arrival. It showed 7:35. She had checked in around 4:00, so she'd been asleep more than three hours.

That's okay, she thought. *I really needed it.* She was now aware of two other needs: having to pee, and a deep hunger for food. The hotel clerk had informed her that each floor had two bathrooms, one at each end of the hall, that served for everyone on that floor.

"But I've placed you on a floor with only one other person, an older lady from the U.K. who's at the other end of the hall. You should have plenty of privacy."

"Thank you," Nia had replied. "That's very kind of you."

"No problem. I know how much you Americans value your privacy."

Nia walked down the hall to the restroom. Again she found it to be cleaner than she'd expected. She then took the stairs down to the lobby. There, she asked the same clerk where she could get something to eat.

"I'm supposed to tell you that our hotel restaurant is the finest in town," the elderly clerk said with a smile, "but that's so far from the truth that I doubt you would believe me anyway. Just down the street is a little bistro. My nephew owns it, and I can truthfully say you will be treated well and will enjoy the meal. Please, let him know that Uncle Benyon sent you."

Nia thanked him again. She was feeling better about this adventure than she had during the dream. People were friendly in this area and seemed to honestly care about each other. Then, a vivid image of the poachers attacking Nibanna flashed before her. Well, okay, not everyone in South Africa was friendly, but at least she wouldn't be totally alone on this impossible mission.

Uncle Benyon was true to his word. She found the Black Rose restaurant without any trouble and enjoyed special treatment as one of his referred guests. The food was delectable. Of course, as hungry as she was, a well prepared plate of dog food would have been passable.

After eating, she decided to walk around the area, making sure to keep her bearings so she'd be able to find the hotel once she was done. Once again, it struck her how warm and friendly everyone was, especially compared to her experience in some of the larger cities of America. There, people were often too busy to even bother to look at each other. The pace here felt slower. People actually did look at each other and often greeted her with a smile and a kind word. Despite all that, it didn't take long before she felt the effects of the long flight and change of time zones. Nap or no nap, it was time for bed.

She returned to the hotel, thanked Uncle Benyon for the restaurant recommendation and retired to her room. This time she turned down the bed and removed her clothes before crawling in between the sheets. It took her less than five minutes to fall into a deep sleep.

And, once more she found herself standing on a hill overlooking a vista of African savannah. Below her, a herd of elephants played in a narrow creek, drinking and spraying water on each other. The scene felt serene and calm, so much more pleasant than her last trip. Suddenly, she heard the distant trumpeting of an elephant. She turned in that direction in time to see one of the most beautiful sights of her life. There, on a second hill, stood a solid white elephant with her trunk in the air, silhouetted by the setting sun.

"Who is that?" Nia asked, even though she was alone. In the next instant, she knew exactly who it was, and an inner voice confirmed it. "That's my granddaughter, Thula," the voice of Nibanna said with pride. "Not as she is, but as she will be one day, one of the greatest leaders of all time."

"Well, then, we simply cannot fail, can we?" Nia spoke softly, but with more conviction than she'd ever felt.

"No, we cannot, must not," Nibanna agreed from afar. "Sleep well, my dear friend. Tomorrow is a big day."

MORNING OF HOPE

Nia awoke with the early morning rays of sunshine streaming through the window and across her bed. She stretched and yawned, finally feeling rested for the first time in days. Rested and hopeful, she realized, remembering the dream of a grown Thula leading her family. Was this a dream of what would happen in the future, or just one possible scenario? Whichever it was, it gave her hope and made her feel ready to tackle whatever the day had in store for her and Sherlock.

She padded down to the nearby bathroom, relieved herself and washed her face before returning to her room to finish dressing. She held up the blouse and shorts and stared at them, seeing them in a new light. What a silly outfit. How had she been so gullible as to let the saleslady back in London convince here that this outfit was perfect for Africa? Everyone else she'd seen wore mostly jeans and t-shirts or more traditional outfits of this part of the country. Many of the native women of South Africa wore long skirts and blouses of bright colors, often with a matching headscarf.

After abandoning her one piece of luggage in Boston, she'd even left her original clothes in London, wanting to travel as light as possible, figuring she could tie up this matter in a day or two at the most. *I'm a silly, ignorant girl,* she chided herself. *It's time I grew up,* she added. She'd just finished putting on the shorts when she heard a knock on her door.

"Who's there?" she asked, feeling suddenly vulnerable standing there half-dressed. Had she locked the door when she'd come back from the bathroom?

"It's me, Sherlock, your trusty guide," came the young boy's voice through the door. Nia breathed a sigh of relief.

"Just a minute. I'm still getting dressed."

"That's why I'm here knocking on your door rather than meeting you in the lobby like we'd planned. I have some clothes for you."

"You what? Really? How come?" Nia asked.

"So you will fit in and be more comfortable," came the reply. "I'll leave them here. If you don't like them, you don't have to wear them. I'll meet you downstairs when you're ready."

After a short pause, Nia replied, "Thank you, Sherlock. That's very kind. I'll be sure to pay you back." But the comment was met with silence. She opened the door to find a neatly folded pile of clothes with a pair of comfortable looking shoes on top, but her guide had already disappeared. The clothes fit perfectly, including the shoes. There wasn't a mirror in the room, so she used her cellphone's camera in selfie mode to see how she looked, then, on the spur of the moment, took a picture of herself. Sherlock was right. She felt so much better in the blue jeans and blouse he'd picked out. Comfortable and practical. *And this is how people dress here. What was that old saying my history teacher used to say? "When in Rome, do as the Romans do…" or something like that.*

Feeling more confident as well as comfortable in her new attire, Nia started for the door, then, on a sudden impulse, turned around to gaze around the room and at the bed where she'd laid out her safari outfit, figuring someone else might find a use for it. She pulled her cellphone out and took a picture of where she'd spent her first night by herself in Africa. "Thank you for making me feel comfortable and safe," she said to the room, before closing the door and walking to the stairs.

She met Sherlock in the lobby. He smiled when he saw that she'd chosen his clothes over the London outfit. "You look mahhvelous," he quipped, suddenly sounding a lot like Billy Crystal, one of her father's favorite comedians.

"Thank you, kind sir," Nia replied, curtsying. "And thank you for the clothes. I promise I will pay you back."

Sherlock nodded. "I have the receipt and have added it to my guide fee. Now, shall we go save some lives?"

"Yes, let's."

Nia paid her hotel bill using her father's AMEX card. She was disappointed, though not surprised, to find that Uncle Banyon had been replaced by a young African lady who seemed more interested in being efficient than friendly. After Nia signed for the bill, she and Sherlock walked outside, where Nia found a dilapidated Jeep parked along the curb. It had seen better days, probably fifteen years ago.

"Your carriage awaits," Sherlock said with a wave of one hand.

As Nia opened the passenger door, she looked around. "Where is the driver?"

Why, right here," Sherlock said, pointing to his chest with his thumb. "When you hire Sherlock, you get two-for-one, a guide and driver."

He waited until Nia reluctantly stepped into the vehicle before walking around it to climb into the driver's seat.

"How old are you?" Nia eyed him suspiciously.

"I'll be fourteen in...," he counted on his fingers, "...fourteen months."

Nia made a quick calculation in her head. "Wait, that means you're only twelve, right?"

Sherlock shrugged and then nodded. "Look at you. Not only beautiful and courageous. You're also good at math." He smiled warmly at her. When Nia didn't smile back, he added, "Calm down. It's really not a problem. Once we get outside the city we'll be home free." He turned the key to start the engine. It finally did after the fourth try.

"Well, maybe I should drive...at least until we get outside the city limits," she added.

Sherlock gazed over at her for a second or two before bursting out laughing. "You are a funny one. Girls can't drive." And with that, he ground the gearshift forward and they lurched ahead.

POACHERS MEETING

One of Musa's least favorite household duties was cleaning out the privy in the rear of their home, but at least he'd finally finished the odious job, which meant he wouldn't need to do it again for a couple of weeks. He started toward the house to wash up, when he heard someone approaching up the gravel walkway. *Who could that be?* he wondered, then decided to investigate. He'd been surprised earlier in the morning to find his father already awake and insisting Thabiso fix him breakfast. It was rare for Zunga to be awake before ten or eleven in the morning, preferring to sleep off as much of his hangover from the night before as possible.

Musa tiptoed around the two room shanty that had been his home since birth and watched in surprise as a short, well-muscled man approached. *Why, that's Garai,* Musa thought. *What in the world is he doing here?* While he'd never actually met the man, Garai's reputation was known far and wide as one of the meanest and yet most powerful men in the area. Why would he be visiting his father?

I don't know, but I intend to find out, Musa thought, as he snuck around to the back of the house. Over the years, he'd found the perfect location to eavesdrop. He was careful not to use it too often, but there were times it was critical that he know what his folks were up to, especially his father, who was unpredictable and could explode without warning. Musa crouched under the main room window and placed one ear against the thin wall. Sure enough, he could hear his father and Garai talking almost as clearly as if he were in the room with them.

"Beer?" he heard his father ask, and a moment later, Garai's gravelly voice accepting.

The two were both men of few words, so it didn't take long for them to get to the purpose of the meeting.

"How are the plans coming together?" Garai asked.

"Very well," Zunga replied. "Our last hunt was a good test. It went smoothly. We were in and out before they knew what hit them. My man was right about the timing."

"So, are we ready to proceed with our plans?"

"Almost. I'm just waiting to hear back about the location of the herd and the best time to strike," Zunga said.

"Who is this mystery man you keep referring to?" Garai asked. "I'm beginning to think he's a figment of your imagination. Someone you made up just to increase the mystery and intrigue."

Zunga laughed. "Oh, he's real all right. But I'm like a newsman. I never reveal my sources, even to you, my friend."

Garai grumbled something that Musa couldn't quite catch, then added, more clearly, "Well, he'd better be in touch soon. I can't keep my men on hold forever. They've got families to feed as well, you know."

"Don't worry. It won't be long, and then we'll all be eating from the fat side of the ox. Now, how about a second beer for the road?"

There was a long silence, during which Musa imagined Garai had simply nodded his agreement, but seconds ticked by and Musa started to grow concerned. He'd not heard the sound of the icebox opening.

"What the hell are you doing there?" Zunga's stern voice said from behind him.

Musa swung around to see the angry face of his father glaring at him.

"Nothing, just sitting here," Musa replied weakly.

"You've been listening, haven't you, boy?"

Musa shook his head, but the lump in his throat kept him from speaking.

Zunga reached out and grabbed him by one ear and hauled him to his feet. Musa screamed in pain. "Stop, you're hurting me!"

"Am I, boy? Really? You think this hurts?" Zunga twisted the ear until it felt to Musa like it would come off in his father's hand. "This is nothing compared to the pain you're about to feel. Now, get inside."

"I wasn't doing anything," Musa pleaded.

"So now you're lying to me, is that it? Well, I'll tell you what you've done. You've sealed your fate, you have. I don't care what your mother says. Anyone who's old enough to sneak around spying on others is damn sure old enough to start hunting for his family and tribe. You're coming with me on this next job, and that's the end of it."

BLACK ROCK MOUNTAIN

Zak and Allie met the next morning outside her room to walk over to the dining hall for breakfast.

"How did you sleep?" Zak asked, even though he knew the answer by looking at his friend's tired eyes.

"Not very well. I kept thinking about those poor animals hiding in fear of being murdered."

"Yeah, me too. I hope we find them soon, before the poachers do."

As they climbed the porch steps of the dining hall, they saw Sampson lying there with a big bowl of food and one of water next to him. He'd only nibbled at the food, however. Zak walked over to him and knelt down close so they could talk without attracting attention.

"Not hungry this morning, Sampson?"

"Not really, even though the chow here is quite good. I'm too worried to eat."

"And that's saying something," Zak kidded, then added, "But I understand. Neither of us slept very well for the same reason." He looked around the porch. "Where's Ra-Kit? Is she sleeping in this morning?"

Sampson shook his head, then nodded to his right. "She rose early and headed off in that direction by herself." He pointed to the east. "I offered to go with her, but she told me to stay here. She said something about needing complete silence to do her work."

"What work?" Zak asked.

Sampson turned his head to stare at Zak for a long moment. "You know she's not very good about sharing such details, but I suspect it involves that little bag of 'herbs' she carries around for such times."

"Oh, magic, huh?"

"I suspect so."

"Well, good. I think we could use some of her magic to help find the elephants," Allie, who'd been listening to the conversation, added.

"Yeah, I'll say," Zak agreed, then pointed to the food bowl. "Eat up, Sampson. We'll also need your strength." He rose from his crouching position. "Let's go get some breakfast, Allie. I'm starving."

As the two teenagers walked into the dining hall, Tokabo strolled by on his way to a long table that held a wide selection of breakfast items including bowls of fruit, platters of bacon and sausage, and covered dishes. "I haven't seen your cat this morning," he said, as he passed by. "Have you?"

Zak shook his head. "No, but I'm sure she's okay." *At least I hope she is,* he thought.

"Yeah, well, I sure hope she's not been eaten by the jackals that hang out at the edge of the compound at night."

"Jackals?" Allie asked, a note of concern in her voice.

"Yeah, we've tried to chase them away, but they're drawn to the smell of food…like that cat of yours."

"She can take care of herself," Zak replied, but with a little less certainty than before.

When the two of them had filled their trays with food, they walked over to a table. "That wasn't a very nice thing to say," Allie commented, as she sat down.

"Yeah, I'm not sure I like him very much. For working at a reserve, he doesn't seem to care that much about animals."

Ra-Kit sat at the top of what the locals referred to as Black Rock Mountain, even though it was really just a tall, sloping hill to anyone who'd ever seen a real mountain. She sat, barely breathing, with her eyes closed, though a closer inspection would reveal rapid eye movements under the lids. One might think she was sleeping, but that would be inaccurate. Actually, Ra-Kit wasn't even there on the mountain. Only her physical body remained, in a state of suspended animation. The spirit of Ra-Kit had traveled far away to the Spiritual Frontier, where she sat gazing up at her old friend, Nibanna.

"I tell you, I don't know where they are," Nibanna said, with a note of frustration. "Fear blocks my connection with my family. I've not been able to connect with them for almost two days. The last I knew of their location on Earth was when they were near the old watering hole, but I'm sure they are far from there now."

Ra-Kit nodded. "I know this is a difficult time for you. We're doing everything we can back on Earth to save your loved ones, but we must find them soon, before the poachers do."

"I know, I know," Nibanna replied. "I appreciate your help, and I wish I could offer you more, but until they calm down, I won't know anymore than I do now. I hope that will be soon."

"So do I, my friend, so do I," Ra-Kit said, as she slowly rose to her feet. "When that happens, how will you get a message to me?"

Nibanna thought for a moment before replying. "Through the birds. Pay attention to the birds."

NIA'S ARRIVAL

After an hour of driving over some of the bumpiest and dustiest roads Nia had ever experienced, Sherlock pulled the Jeep through the gate of the Thula Thula Game Reserve's compound and turned off the engine. Nia climbed out, stretched and dusted herself off. *I'm finally here. After over two days of traveling, I'm here!* She looked over to Sherlock, who was also brushing the dust from his pant legs.

"Thanks for getting me here. You really are a good driver. Now, what do I owe you?" Suddenly, she realized she might not have enough cash to pay him. She'd grown accustomed to using credit cards for everything she needed to purchase.

"But, our time together isn't over," Sherlock said. "When your work here is done, you'll need a ride back into town. I'll just hang out here in the meantime. I have a few friends that work here that I've not seen in quite awhile. It will be good to reconnect with them."

"Are you sure?"

"Yeah, no problem. Take your time. Save some animals. I'll be here when you're ready to go home."

"That's very kind of you," Nia replied. As Sherlock headed toward the main building, Nia began to look around. "Where is everyone?" But even as she spoke the words, she saw a small group coming around the corner of one of the buildings toward her, including one of the largest black dogs she'd ever seen. Next to him was a young boy she immediately recognized from her previous internet research.

"It's Zak! Zak Bates!" she exclaimed, excited to see someone she knew even though they'd never met. It felt good to see a familiar face when she was so far from home.

The boy stopped suddenly and the girl walking behind him bumped into him. "It's the girl that's been stalking me!"

"What? Who?" the girl asked, looking around and finally resting her gaze on Nia.

"There." Zak pointed at Nia. "She's the one I told you about."

"Oh, yeah. I remember." Nia could feel the girl's gaze running up and down her body. "You're right. She is pretty."

"Yeah, I know. That's what's so strange about it. I've never had a pretty girl stalk me before."

"Hey, wait a minute," Nia blurted out, as she approached them. "I wasn't stalking you. I was just trying to get someone to help me." She paused. "So, you think I'm pretty?"

"What?! Wait." Zak's face turned red. "I...I..."

"Never mind," the other girl said, stepping forward. "Boys are so silly." She held out her hand. "I'm Allie George. What's your name?"

"Nia Gaines. Pleased to meet you." They shook hands. "And could that be Sampson, by any chance?" she asked, nodding in the black dog's direction.

"Yeah. You have done your research, haven't you?" Allie replied. "Are you sure you're not a stalker after all?"

There was a long pause before the two girls burst out laughing. When Nia stopped giggling, she said, "No, I was just desperate to find someone who could help me, and I ran across Zak's blog. I read one of the stories, but I had no idea that there was a real Sampson."

"Well, you know how writers borrow from their real life," Zak finally found the ability to talk again. "Of course, the rest of it is all made up. Sampson can't really fly and there aren't such things as magic cats."

"Of course not," Nia agreed. She turned to Sampson. "Still, it's a pleasure to meet you. You don't mean to tell me that your cat is here as well?"

"Yeah, she's around here somewhere. It's a long story how this came about," Zak added. "Too long to explain now. Let's just be thankful that we're all together. We have a family of elephants that need our help."

"That's so true," Nia agreed, then, on a sudden impulse, she stepped forward and gave Zak a big hug while Allie looked on. They stood there for several seconds, with Zak's face growing even redder than it had before.

"Ahh, I think we better get a move on," Allie finally said, stepping forward in an attempt to separate her best friend from this overly friendly and way too pretty girl.

"Yeah, you're right," Nia said, as she stepped back but continued to hold Zak's hand. "I just know we're all going to be such good friends."

Allie stopped walking and watched as Nia grasped Zak's elbow and the two strolled away to find David and Tokabo. *Who does this Nia girl think she is, storming in here and taking over like this? Look at them. It's like they're walking into their prom night or something.* She didn't know what was going on, but one thing she did know. She didn't like the feeling that came over her when seeing her best friend and this pretty girl together.

Tokabo leaned back against the wall of the veranda, placing himself further into the shadows. He watched as yet another unexpected and unannounced teenager arrived. What was going on here? He didn't know the answer to that, but whatever it was, it couldn't be good. The more people around, the more chance that something could go wrong. He glanced around to be sure no one was watching him, then pulled out his cellphone. As much as he hated making the call, he knew the repercussions of not doing sol could be far worse. He didn't trust his sister's husband to not have someone watching the watcher, so he punched in the numbers and waited, but this time the call was redirected to voicemail.

"This is Zunga. Leave a message," and a beep. Funny, even that short a message annoyed Tokabo. He hesitated. *Maybe I should just hang up.* But then he remembered that his number would be left on the other phone. Besides, this way he might avoid having to actually talk to the man.

"It's me doing my job as you ordered." *Watch the tone there big guy. This is not someone you want to piss off.* "We've just had another unexpected arrival. This one is also a teenager, a girl who looks to be around sixteen. We need to get moving on this deal if we're going to do it. Too many people showing up here. What if they start getting nosy? I know you need to know the location of the animals, and I'm doing my best to find out, but you better have everything ready to go at your end." Suddenly emboldened by leaving the message, he added, "Also, this is it for me. Once this job is done, I'm out of here. You'll have to find someone else to do your dirty work." He disconnected the call.

That felt good, he thought. *It's about time I stood up for myself. Now what? Time to go find Dr. Dondi.* She was his best bet for finding the location of the elephant herd. Besides, she was probably over at the animal hospital taking care of the sick and injured animals. It would feel good to help her out.

He found Dr. Dondi changing the bandages on a young zebra that had a nasty gash on one leg. He stepped in to help hold the animal, which wasn't too happy to be restrained. After a couple minutes, he broached the question on his mind.

"Any luck locating the herd?"

"Nope, but I plan to go out again later this afternoon," Dr. Dondi replied. "You want to tag along?"

"Sure, why not. Wouldn't hurt to have another pair of eyes up there."

"Exactly," Dr. Dondi agreed. "Okay, that should do it. You can let him go." She turned to Tokabo. "You know, you're really good with animals. Have you ever thought of going to vet school or at least being trained as a vet tech?"

"Nah," Tokabo replied, suddenly embarrassed. "Too much schooling for my taste. I'll just keep doing what I'm doing."

But as she walked away, the words kept reverberating in his mind. *Yeah, doing what I'm doing...helping a bunch of ruthless poachers kill innocent elephants because I'm too much of a coward to do anything about it.* The thought made him feel worse than ever. He started towards the bunkhouse. *Time for a drink, maybe a couple of them.*

MUSA'S HOME LIFE

Musa sat on the carved log his father and he had dragged from the woods years ago before Zunga discovered the numbing power of alcohol. Spending time with his father turning the lump of wood into a work of art was one of Musa's favorite memories about his father. He held on to it like a cherished jewel. Today, he watched his mother performing her own form of artistic joy as she danced around Miriando, an elderly lady that had been coming to Thabiso for as long as Musa could remember for both physical and spiritual healing. He was proud of his mother's role in the village as one of the youngest and most powerful sangomas. Sangomas were often misidentified by foreigners as "witch doctor" but the name couldn't be further from the truth. Sangomas cared for the village's physical, emotional, and spiritual illnesses or disturbances.

Today, Thabiso vigorously danced around Miriando in an effort to drive out a spirit that had disturbed the old lady's ability to sleep. This had led to her being 'ornery as a hornet' according to her husband, who had insisted she go see her spiritual guide.

While Musa didn't understand how his mother's power worked, it certainly appeared to be having a positive effect on her patient, who stood in the center of their small, well manicured backyard with her eyes closed and a blissful look on her face.

Thabiso made one last circle around her, singing with a high-pitched keening and a vigorous waving of her arms, which Musa recognized to be her equivalent of an encore performance. As she dropped to the ground, one hand caught in the brightly colored beads of her long necklace and the gems flew in every direction.

Musa rose to his feet, tempted to applaud, but refrained. He'd learned that such behavior was frowned upon by the spirits, or at least that's what his mother had told him the one time he'd done it. "Ahh, Maama, you broke your favorite necklace," Musa said, stepping forward to help her up.

"Oh, no matter," Thabiso replied, wiping the perspiration from her forehead. "I have plenty more."

"Yes, you do," Musa said. "You love making your jewelry."

"Indeed I do, despite your father's attempt to stop me. Please pick up any of the stones you can find so I can save them for another piece, while I finish up with Miriando."

Musa did as she asked, then waited to hand them over until his mother returned. "I've heard you and father argue several times in the past about how much time you spend with your jewelry making, but not recently. How come?" Musa asked, as he dropped the last of the gems into Thabiso's hands.

"Well, I finally had to draw a line as to what orders of his I would take and which I wouldn't," Thabiso replied, with a wiry smile. "You have to know when and where to pick your battles, Musa. Besides, I convinced your father that an evil spirit would descend upon our village if I stopped making jewelry."

"Really? Is that true?"

"Well, let's just say it served its purpose, and leave it at that." His mother rubbed his head and, with a flurry of her wide skirt, twirled around to enter their home.

TRIP TO TOWN

The three teenagers, followed closely behind by Sampson, went looking for David to find out what next steps he had planned to find and protect the elephants. They found him finishing up a conversation with Donna and Tokabo.

"You two take the helicopter out and see if you can locate the herd. I'm heading into town on another matter." As the two nodded and headed off, David turned to the teens.

"Who's your new friend?" he asked, as he stepped forward and offered Nia his hand.

"This is Nia Gaines," Zak replied. "She's from the States as well, and is our newest Eco-adventure Team member."

"What?!" Allie blurted out. "Since when?"

Zak ignored her outburst. "She's here to help us save Thula."

"Well, glad to have you. We have to find her first, but I have a plan for when we do."

"Is that why you're heading into town?" Zak asked.

"Yes, that's right. I need to meet a lady who specializes in getting rid of vermin like these poachers. Her name is Kinessa Newman. I've never met her, but she has a reputation for being one tough character. She's former U.S. Military."

"She sounds like a badass," Zak said. "Can we come with you?"

"Sure, I don't see why not. Let me just get a few bottles of water and I'll meet you at the Land Rover."

Zak turned to Allie. "You and Sampson stay here in case Ra-Kit shows up. Come on, Nia. Let's go meet Kinessa-badass."

"Wait just a minute," Allie objected. "Why can't Sampson stay here on his own and look for Ra-Kit?"

"Don't be silly," Zak replied. "He's just a dog, and you know dogs and cats don't always get along, even though these two usually manage to work things out. Besides, I need you to let me know when she returns."

Zak and Nia walked away, with Nia occasionally touching Zak's arm, leaving a fuming Allie behind. Once they were out of earshot, Sampson came over and stood next to her. "It'll all be okay," he assured her.

"Will it?" Allie asked, turning to him. "I'm not so sure about our new 'team member'. She seems awfully touchy-feely to me."

David met Zak and Nia at the Land Rover with the keys in hand. The three of them climbed in. As they started to drive off, Tokabo walked out of the garage.

"Where you headed to, boss?"

David stopped the vehicle. "Into town to meet someone about this poaching problem."

"Oh, yeah? Who's that?"

"Woman by the name of Kinessa Newman. She runs a security agency. You know her?"

Tokabo shook his head and frowned. "Never heard of her. Security agency, huh? Seems kinda extreme measures to me. Don't you think we can handle matters ourselves?"

"We might have to," David agreed. "But she comes highly recommended, so I'm going to at least meet with her."

Tokabo nodded slowly. "Just seems like we're getting too many cooks in this here kitchen, if you ask me, but you didn't, so I'll stay out of it." He tapped the side of the Rover to send them on their way. It seemed to Zak that he'd put a lot more force behind it than necessary. *Probably just having a bad day,* he thought. After all, everyone was worried about the elephants. As they pulled onto the main road, Zak glanced behind him. Through the dust, he could see Tokabo returning to the garage, his cellphone in hand. *Who was he calling this time?*

Before Nia knew it, she was bouncing back down the road she'd just come up with Sherlock less than an hour before, but this time the trip seemed a lot more fun with Zak beside her. She found his enthusiasm and positive energy infectious. Besides, she liked that he thought she was pretty and had readily accepted her as part of the team.

"This is exciting, isn't it?" Zak said, as he gazed out the window at a herd of water buffalo grazing in a nearby field. "I've not been to the town yet. What's it called?"

"Ntambanana," Nia replied, grasping the strap over her head to steady herself.

"What a funny name."

"Hey, wait a minute," Nia said. "If you haven't been there before, how did you get to the reserve?"

Zak didn't answer at first, but his eyes darted around as though looking for the right thing to say. "Ahh, it's a little complicated. Let's just say we had special transportation provided." He sat forward in his seat and tapped David on the shoulder. "What do you know about this Kinessa lady?"

"Not a lot, which is why I want to meet her, but I have a friend who hired her a couple years ago when he was having security issues. When I described our problem, he recommended her. Said that if anyone could handle the issue, she could."

Zak nodded and sat back in his seat. Nia was about to ask him again about the 'special transportation', when he pointed out the window at a flock of flamingos flying by. "Wow! Aren't they magnificent? Isn't Africa just the most wondrous place you've ever seen?"

Nia nodded and decided to drop the question for now. Still, she had a feeling there was more to Zak and his team than met the eye. She remembered the story she'd read on his blog. Could more of it have been true than she'd first thought? *No way. I mean really, a flying dog and a magic cat? That's pure fantasy. Right?* The two of them remained silent for the rest of the trip, enjoying the passing scenery and the wildlife that inhabited it.

In less time than Nia had anticipated, they entered the village of Ntambanana and David pulled the Land Rover over to the side of the road in front of an office building with a sign that read simply: *Newman's Security*. The three of them climbed out and David led the way. As they entered the building, Nia was first struck by the two glass cases along one wall, each filled with an assortment of rifles and handguns. *What an arsenal,* she thought.

At the far end of the room, a young woman sat behind a desk dressed in a military green blouse and pants. The short sleeves revealed two muscular arms with an assortment of tattoos on each. As they approached, the woman looked up from her paperwork, smiled confidently at David and rose from her chair, then came around to shake his hand.

"David Shedrick, I presume. I'm Kinessa Newman. Pleased to meet you." She glanced over at Zak and Nia. "Are these your children?"

"Oh, no," David replied with a chuckle. "I'm not married."

"Really? That's interesting," Kinessa said, with a smile that transformed her stern face to one that bordered between pretty and beautiful. "That makes two of us." She held his hand for just a moment longer before letting go of it.

"These two are here from the U.S. to do what they can to help save the reserve's herd of elephants." He introduced Zak and Nia.

"I see. All the way from America. How interesting," Kinessa replied. "Please, have a seat. What can I do for you?"

"Well, as I explained over the phone, we're having problems with poachers. Just yesterday, they snuck onto the reserve's land and killed two of our magnificent males, butchered them for the ivory, and escaped before we could do anything. I'm at my wit's end as to what to do. A friend of mine recommended you."

"I understand," Kinessa replied. Her face returned to a stern look bordering on anger. "Poachers are the scum of the earth. They rank right up there with terrorists and sex traffickers. I've made it my personal mission to rid this country of every poacher before I'm finished. You've come to the right place. It will be my pleasure to take care of the matter."

"And what do you intend to do?" David asked.

"That's simple. I plan to set a trap just like they often do. I'll treat them just like the animals they are…"

"And then?"

"Why, kill them, of course," Kinessa said matter of factly.

"Really? Isn't that a bit extreme?" Zak asked. "Couldn't you set a trap to capture them and turn them over to the authorities?"

"In this part of the country, I am the authorities -- at least the only authority they understand. You see, Zak, in a situation like this, you've got to fight fire with fire. These poachers are lawless men that know only one thing -- violence, so you fight them with violence. Besides, most of the 'authorities' around here are corrupt. If we turned the poachers over to them, it wouldn't be any time before they'd be out killing again. No, leave it to me. I know. This is the only way to handle this matter once and for all."

Zak glanced over to Nia, who wore a distressed look on her face, and then to David, who seemed unperturbed by it all. "And how much do you charge for such services, Ms. Newman?" David asked.

"That's the best part of this whole thing. It'll cost you nothing."

David stared at her, a look of doubt on his face. "Come again?"

"No charge," Kinessa repeated. "You see, almost every one of these poachers has a price on his head. I just have a simple form for you to sign that I keep all the reward money."

"In that case, I say we have a deal," David replied, sticking out his hand. Kinessa took it in her own and the two shook on it. She reached into her desk drawer and pulled out a sheet of paper.

"Just sign here, and we're all set. I'll be out in a couple of days, once I line up my men."

David took the paper from her, read over it, and was about to sign it when Zak spoke up. "Wait a minute. Are you sure this is the best approach?"

"Yeah," Nia agreed. "This all seems extreme to say the least. Maybe we should start by reporting the poachers to the real authorities. Surely there must be someone who's not corrupt."

David looked at Zak and then Nia. "I'm sorry, but I've done that in the past, and Kinessa is right. It made no difference. This is the best way, the only way I see to proceed." He placed the paper on the desk in front of him and signed it before handing it back to her. They shook hands again.

"I'll get right on this," Kinessa said, as she took the paper from him and slid it into a desk drawer. "Don't worry, kids. You can head on home now. Everything is in good hands." She turned to David. "And I'll see you in a couple of days."

"Right-o," David replied. As they headed toward the exit, he pulled out his cellphone. "Wait just a second, guys." He punched in the number and waited for someone at the other end to pick up. "Hey, Tokabo. The meeting went well, very well." He waited for Tokabo to say something before continuing. "Yeah, well, I'm in charge, so the buck stops with me. If this goes wrong, it'll be on me. I just called to tell you to be sure the spare bunk house is clean and ready to go. We'll have several more visitors staying with us in a couple of days."

He disconnected the phone, but stared at it for a moment. "Not sure what's gotten into him lately. He's been snarky with me of late. I might have to talk to him about it." He turned back to Zak and Nia. "Okay, let's head home."

Tokabo stuck the phone back in his hip pocket. Kinessa and her men would be arriving in a couple of days and then it would be impossible for Zunga to continue with his plans. *Maybe I should just let things run their course. What are the chances that he'd ever find out that I withheld a little information like that? But what if he did somehow?* It was way too risky. Not only would he be putting himself in danger, but also his sister and nephew. *But first,* he thought, *I have to offset the bad news with some good news. I've got to find those elephants.*

He jogged in the direction of the helipad, where he found Dr. Dondi and the pilot getting ready to take off.

"I was just about to call you," Dr. Dondi said. "Ready to go look for that herd?"

"Better than that," Tokabo replied. "I'm ready to find them."

"That's the spirit." She gave him a high five. "I'm a little surprised you accepted my invitation. I thought you told me you didn't like to fly."

Tokabo nodded. "Not my favorite pastime for sure, but I figure the best way to get over my fear is to meet it head on. Let's do it."

The two of them climbed into the Sikorsky S-76C and, after a last minute safety check, the pilot gave a thumbs up and they were off.

Tokabo felt his stomach do a backflip as the chopper soared to the left. What had he gotten himself into this time? They sure better find the elephants on this trip. Time was running out, as was his courage.

Dr. Dondi pointed to the headset she wore and then to a second set for him to put on. After he'd adjusted them, he heard her say, "This way we can talk to each other without having to yell our heads off.

"And, we can talk to the pilot," she added. "Frankie, let's head over to the southern side of the reserve. We haven't checked that area yet."

The pilot nodded and turned the helicopter due south, and once more Tokabo felt a wave of nausea course through him. *It's going to be a long afternoon,* he thought, but, fortunately, for once he was wrong.

They'd only been flying a little over an hour when he thought he saw something to his right out the side window. He tapped Dr. Dondi on the shoulder and pointed. She glanced in that direction, then nodded.

"Frankie, over to our right, how about it?"

This time the redirection was much gentler. Either that or his stomach was finally adjusted to the conditions.

"That's them!" Dr. Dondi exclaimed a minute later. "We found them!" She turned and gave Tokabo another high five.

"Not too close, Frankie. We don't want to spook them. They're really something to see, even from this distance, aren't they?"

Tokabo nodded, but once again, he felt sick to his stomach, and not from the motion of the helicopter. In a day or two, several of these magnificent beasts would be lying dead on the ground with their bodies mutilated, and it would be his fault.

"Boy, won't David and the kids be excited. I'll radio it in."

But before she could do so, Tokabo reached over and stilled her hand. "Let's wait until we get back," he urged. He leaned over in his seat closer to the doctor. "Some funny things have been going on around here. I'm not sure, but I think we may have a snitch in our midst."

"Really? Who?" Dr. Dondi asked, a look of surprise on her face.

"I'm not sure, and until I am, I think it's best we keep this to ourselves. I'll tell David later this evening when we get back, but for now, let's just keep it among the four of us. What do you say?"

"Yeah, well, if you think that's what we should do."

"I do," Tokabo replied. "Just for a day or two." *By that time it won't matter who knows. The deed will have been done and the snitch will be long gone from these parts.*

TOWN SQUARE

As the three companions left Kinessa's office, they heard a commotion down the street, the sound of music and people clapping. "What's that?" Zak asked.

"Sounds like it's coming from the square," David replied. "Do you want to go check it out?"

"Sure," Nia replied.

"I guess," Zak added reluctantly.

"Come on. It'll be fun," David said, as he waved the other two to join him.

Nia took Zak's hand and together they followed David down the street. They approached an open area lined with small shops and restaurants. In the center a group of locals stood around clapping to the music as a young boy stood in the center dancing. The three of them made their way slowly to the front and watched for several seconds as the boy twisted and turned to the music in what appeared to be a spontaneous dance routine made up in the moment.

"He's good," David said.

"I'll say," Nia replied, raising her voice to be heard over the music. "He's more than good. He's excellent."

The three continued watching as the music slowly changed to a slower tempo and the dancer adjusted to the change. Then the music started to pick up again and so did the boy, his dreadlocks flowing around his face. After another minute or two, Nia pulled her wallet out of her pocket and pulled out a twenty dollar bill.

Seeing that she was about to put it in the hat where several other people had already deposited money, David grasped her hand to stop her. Leaning over so she could hear him, he said, "Do you want to start a riot? That's too much."

"But he's that good," she replied.

"Well, if you want to be that generous, wait until he finishes and give it to him personally."

Nia nodded and put the bill away in her pocket. When the music finally finished, the crowd clapped and cheered, and the sweaty dancer smiled and bowed before heading over to the hat to collect his money. David made his way through the crowd, with Zak and Nia following him. As they approached the dancer, Nia took the lead.

"You were amazing!" she exclaimed, jumping up and down with excitement. "I'm Nia, and this is Zak and David." She pointed to her two friends.

"I'm Musa," the dancer said with a smile. "Sorry, my English, it's not good."

"No problem. I understand you perfectly," Nia replied. She reached into her pocket and pulled out the twenty dollar bill. "I want you to have this." She placed it in the palm of Musa's hand and wrapped his fingers around it. "It's for you only," she added. "May I ask you about a couple of your dance moves?"

Musa nodded. He glanced at the bill in his hand and his eyes widened. "You may ask me anything, my new American friend."

Zak elbowed David standing next to him. "She seems to make friends wherever she goes."

"That's true," David replied. "Jealous?"

"Who, me? Well, yes, maybe just a little."

"Well, I wouldn't be," David replied. "She seems to have taken a shine to you already."

Nia and Musa chatted for several minutes about their mutual love of dancing. Musa struggled a bit with the language barrier, but they'd found a second common language they both understood -- dance. Musa was just finishing showing her one of his original dance steps when he stopped in mid turn. He stared off in the distance for a second before turning back to Nia.

"I must go. So sorry." He turned to leave, then stopped. "Thank you." He glanced again in the same direction as before, a look of fear growing on his face.

"Wait!" David exclaimed. "What's wrong?" He looked in the same direction in time to see a large man with a nasty scar on his face pushing his way through the crowd. "Do you know that man?" He turned back to Musa, but the boy had already disappeared.

"Who is that?" Zak asked.

"One of the meanest men I've ever met," David replied. "Well, to be honest, we've never been formerly introduced, but I had a run in with him a few years ago. After that, I did a little poking around. His name is Zunga. He heads up a gang of thugs. In fact, I wouldn't be surprised if it's his gang that slaughtered our elephants the other day." He looked in the direction where Musa and the man had disappeared and then snapped his fingers.

"What?" Zak asked.

"I just figured it out," David replied. "That boy must be Zunga's son. He's about the right age, and for sure they knew each other."

"No," Nia replied. "That can't be. I mean, Musa's a dancer, not a killer."

David frowned. "Unfortunately, one doesn't preclude the other. There are plenty of talented people in the world who aren't all good. But that's okay." He held up his cellphone. "I've got a picture of the boy, and I know where I can get photos of his father. Kinessa will handle this. I have no doubt. Let's get going."

Zak and Nia stared at each other. Noticing the distress on Nia's face, Zak tried to comfort her. "It'll be alright," he said, though the words sounded hollow even to him.

"No, it won't," Nia replied angrily. "This is all going bad. I wish I'd never come to Africa," she said, stomping away.

RA-KIT RETURNS

Sampson sat at the edge of the reserve's compound staring in the direction of Black Rock Mountain, watching as the sun continued to set behind it. With each passing moment, his worry grew. It wasn't like Ra-Kit hadn't gone on similar walkabouts in the past, but this one felt different. For one thing, the stakes were higher than ever before, so it was even more important that she be available to lend her magical powers to the mission. Plus, well, the truth was Ra-Kit wasn't getting any younger. None of them were, and while that was fine for Zak and Allie, who were still growing into their own powers as young adults, Sampson and Ra-Kit were on the other end of that spectrum.

Where is all this coming from? Sampson thought. For sure, he didn't feel old. If anything, he felt more vigorous and able to deal with life than ever before, in part because Ra-Kit was sharing some of her powers with him. He was still contemplating these matters when he noticed a small figure slowly drawing nearer. Finally, his lifelong companion had returned. When Ra-Kit was close enough to hear, he stood up. "It's about time you came back."

Ra-Kit continued walking toward him, ignoring the comment.

"Did you hear what I said?" Sampson asked. As she passed him, he fell in step beside her.

"I heard," Ra-Kit replied. Sampson could tell from the sound of her voice that it had been a long day for her, which meant that if she was tired, she'd also be ornery, more so than usual. *Tread lightly,* he warned himself.

"It's just that I was worried about you," Sampson continued. "There are wild animals out there."

Ra-kit stopped and looked at him. "Do you honestly think they'd mess with me?"

Before Sampson could reply, the sound of a vehicle interrupted their conversation. "That must be David and the kids returning from town," Sampson said. "Let's go see what they found out." Ra-Kit nodded.

"Would you like a ride?" Sampson asked.

Ra-Kit nodded again. "That would be most kind, my friend."

Sampson lowered himself so she could climb onto his shoulders, and the two headed towards the compound. As Sampson walked, he noticed the mounting clouds off in the distance. *It looks like we might get some rain in the next day or two.* Storms at this time of the year weren't all that common, but when they did occur, they were often real gushers. It was not uncommon for the area to receive several inches in just a couple hours.

As they approached the Land Rover, Zak and Nia climbed out, then David drove off to take the vehicle to be filled with gas. Allie came out of the dining hall to join them.

"About time you got home," she said. "Did you two have a good time in town?" The edge of jealousy in her voice was unmistakable.

"Oh, yes," Nia replied, apparently unperturbed by it. "I met the nicest boy. His name is Musa, and he's an incredible dancer. Only, David says that he and his dad are part of the gang of poachers." She turned to Zak. "Listen, I'm going to clean up before dinner. I feel like I've inhaled a lungful of dust in the last few hours. I'll see you at dinner." Once again, she touched Zak on the arm. "Thanks for inviting me to come with you today." She walked away towards the barracks.

After she'd left, Allie turned to Zak. "How did it go?"

Zak brought the rest of the team up to date on David's decision to hire Kinessa and her security team.

"They're to be out in a day or two," Zak finished. "David seems convinced it's the only way. He says it's time to fight fire with fire."

"That's unfortunate," Ra-Kit said from where she sat on Sampson's shoulders. "My experience of fighting fire with fire is that a lot of people, and sometimes animals, get burned."

Zak and Allie nodded. "Well, let's all get washed up for dinner. I think we could all use a good night's sleep," Zak said. He turned to Allie. "And what did you do today?"

"As if you cared," she replied, and turned to enter her own building.

Zak stood there, befuddled by the remark. "What did I do now?" He directed the question to Sampson and Ra-Kit.

"You've a lot to learn about dealing with the opposite sex," Sampson replied.

"Yes, he does," Ra-Kit agreed, "but now is not the time for that lesson. Take me to the room."

The two animals walked away, leaving Zak behind to sort it out the best he could.

DOUBLE SUNRISE

Zak and the rest of the team retired early that night, but once in his room, Zak found sleeping was not so easy. Instead, he tossed and turned, fighting with his pillow and sheet in an effort to get comfortable. He finally drifted off, only to awake a few hours later with a stomach ache. *I knew I shouldn't have eaten that third slice of pie, but it was just so good.* In fact, the meals they served at the reserve were some of the best he'd had anywhere. He climbed out of bed and dropped to the floor to do a round of pushups. He was trying to work up to fifty at a time, but so far, the best he could do was twenty-five. Tonight, he wasn't interested in beating his all time record but simply trying to tire himself out so he could sleep. It worked. When he returned to bed, he managed to drift off within a few minutes.

He awoke after a few hours again and glanced at his phone for the time. It read 5:45. The sun would be rising soon. He climbed out of bed and went to the window. He thought he could see the first signs of light off on the horizon. *Another magical day in Africa,* he thought. At least he hoped it would be magical and not monstrous. Thula's herd was still missing and the poachers as well. Kinessa and her security force would be arriving later in the morning. Yes, a monstrous day seemed more likely than magical. Still, there was Ra-Kit and Sampson, two animals with special talents when it came to magic. All was not lost, not by a long shot.

He decided to go ahead and get dressed. It wouldn't be long before the dining hall would open and he could go get breakfast. Funny, just a few hours ago he felt like he might not ever be hungry again, and here he was thinking about the next meal already. After putting on his clothes, he walked over to the window and looked out again. Yep, definitely a lightening of the sky was happening, but something wasn't right about it.

He didn't recall being able to see the sun rise from his room. Didn't the sun rise in the other direction? He slipped on his tennis shoes and had started toward the door to go investigate this mystery when he heard the first cry, which sent a shudder of fear coursing through his body.

"Fire!"

He ran back to the window. The orange glow he'd mistaken for the rising sun was much more prominent now. As the sky continued to lighten from the rising sun on the other side of the barracks, he thought he could just make out the first signs of a smoke trail as well. He flew to the door and pulled on the handle to open it. It pulled in slightly, but then stopped. He pulled harder but still couldn't open it. He put his eye up to the slit in the doorway and could just make out a rope binding the outer doorknob to the wood column across the way. Someone had tied the door closed, but why? Well, there was more than one way out of his room. He returned to the window. As he reached to open it, a vaguely uncomfortable feeling arose. He tried pulling the lower part of the window open, but once again found he was unable to budge it. He checked the lock above it. It was unlocked. *But wasn't the window open when I first arrived?* Sure it was. It had been warm that night and he remembered enjoying the cool breeze blowing in from the window. But now, not only was it closed, it wouldn't open even though it was unlocked. Someone didn't want him going outside his room, and had turned it into a small jail cell.

He could hear a flurry of activity outside as the warning of fire was repeated a number of times. He felt a wave of panic building inside. What if the fire in the distance wasn't the only fire? What if whoever had started that fire had decided to start one closer to home, like in the next building or even in this one? What if Allie's and Nia's building had also been set on fire? He frantically glanced around the room for a way out. His gaze fell on the straight back chair he'd used to pile his clothes on for the last two nights. *There's more than one way out of this room,* he thought again. He dragged the chair over to the window, then picked it up over his head, suddenly thankful for all the hundreds of pushups he'd done over the last few weeks. He flung the chair through the window, shards of glass flying in all directions. Once again, he could feel the cool breeze of morning wafting through the window's opening. He pulled the sheet off his bed and wrapped it around his hand. He used it to clear the remaining pieces of glass out of the way, then laid the sheet over the wooden frame before climbing out. As he ran toward the other barracks building, he noticed he wasn't the only one running around in the early morning light. Chaos had arrived at the reserve in the form of a real live fire.

But where is the rest of my team? He glanced back to the shattered window and the glass strewn on the ground around the fallen chair. Whoever wanted him locked in his room probably didn't want the rest of the Eco-adventure Team getting in the way either. He ran around the building to the second set of barracks. Sure enough, both girls' doors had been securely tied shut. He could hear pounding coming from both. He pulled his pocket knife out and went to work on the rope securing Allie's door. As the last strand separated, the door flew open.

"What in the world in going on?" a red-faced Allie asked, as she rushed out.

"There's a fire there in the distance," Zak explained, pointing. "And whoever set it didn't want us to get in the way of their plans. Go find Ra-Kit and Sampson. They've probably been locked in as well." As Allie ran off in the direction of the animal compound, where injured animals were often housed and where David had quartered Ra-Kit and Sampson, Zak moved on to cut the ropes securing Nia's door.

"Stop beating on the door," he yelled to her. "Just give me another minute and you'll be free."

"Is that you, Zak?" a desperate sounding Nia asked.

"At your service," Zak replied, as he sawed on the rope.

A moment later, the door flung open and an elated Nia threw her arms around him and gave him a big smooch on the side of his face. "Thank you, thank you! I thought I'd never get out of there."

Before Zak could do anything, Allie appeared from around the corner with Sampson and Ra-Kit following behind. "Well, if you two aren't just so sweet," she said sarcastically. "Maybe this isn't the best time for hugging and kissing."

"I wasn't...I mean, it's not..." Zak stammered, pulling Nia's arm from around him.

"Never mind that now. We have a fire to get to," Allie replied, cutting him off.

"What? Fire? Where?" Nia asked, disregarding Allie's comment.

"Over there," Zak replied. As he did so, two Land Rovers and a Jeep drove by at an alarming speed, trailing a cloud of dust behind them. Zak could just make out David driving the lead car and he wasn't sure, but it looked like Tokabo driving the second car.

"They're heading to the fire," Allie said.

"And leaving us behind," Zak added.

"Well, there's the Jeep that Sherlock used to drive me here," Nia said. "It's around back. Has anyone seen him?"

"You mean the little kid with the strange hat? No, I haven't seen him. Why?"

"Well, he knows how to drive. He's quite good at it. Unfortunately, I don't drive. My family has a chauffeur..." Nia stopped, suddenly embarrassed to continue.

"No worry," Zak said. "I'll drive. Let's go."

They arrived at the Jeep winded, all except Ra-Kit, who rode on Sampson's back. Zak ran around to the driver's seat while Sampson and Ra-Kit jumped in the back. Allie and Nia both tried to take the passenger seat next to Zak, but Allie finally won out, leaving Nia to climb in the back with the two animals.

"When did you learn to drive?" Allie asked, putting on her seatbelt.

"About five minutes from now," Zak replied. He looked around for the key, finally finding it under the floorboard mat. He stuck it into the ignition, but stopped when he noticed the stick shift between the seats and the extra pedal on the floor. He groaned.

"What's wrong?" Allie asked.

"It has a manual transmission."

"What does that mean?" Nia asked from the backseat.

"Let's just say it's not as easy to drive." *Like next to impossible,* Zak thought. His brother had tried to show him how once in the school parking lot, but finally gave up after Zak jerked the car around, stalling out a half dozen times.

"What do we do?" Allie asked, her voice becoming more frantic.

Before Zak could answer, they heard a shout from behind them.

"Hey! What are you doing with my Jeep? Get out of there!"

"Thank, God. It's Sherlock," Nia said, waving at the boy, who still wore her Pith helmet cocked to one side.

"Oh, hi, Nia. I didn't recognize you. What's up?"

"We've got to go save the elephants, but no one knows how to drive this thing," Nia explained.

"Well, scoot on over," Sherlock said, directing the comment to Zak. "After all, I'm your driver." He smiled at Nia.

There was a scrambling around as Zak started to climb in the backseat only to be pulled back to the passenger seat by Allie, who then joined Nia and the animals.

"Hang on, everyone," Sherlock instructed, as he turned the key in the ignition and the Jeep roared to life on only the second try.

"The Eco-adventure Team is on the move!" Zak shouted, waving his arm in the air and pointing in the direction of the fire.

THULA IN CRISIS

I'm tired, Mama. I think I'm going to lie down for just a little while.
Nandi felt Thula move beneath her to rest in her shadow.

Nandi nudged her baby. *No, Thula, don't. You mustn't. Stay standing. Lean on me, my precious.*

But we've been walking for so long.

Yes, I know but it won't be much longer. Look, up ahead. It's Synda and Obeka come to join us.

Nandi felt Thula stumble, then catch herself. *But I'm so tired. My legs hurt. Please, just a little rest. I promise I'll stand when they...*

No, hold on. They are almost here, and look, they have something for you, for both of us.

The two aunts approached, ecstatic to find their missing family members still alive. One held the limb of a Baobab tree with its fruit dangling from it while the other held a long strip of the tree's succulent bark. The tree was known by the locals as the Tree of Life and for good reason. As a succulent, it was able to absorb and store water during the rainy season, then later produce a nutrient-dense fruit in the dry season.

Synda lay the branch before her leader and bowed. Nandi touched the top of her head in thanks before reaching down and taking one of the fruits in her trunk.

How far is it? she asked, as she put a second fruit in her mouth.

Not far, Obeka assured her. *Just over that ridge.*

Can you make it that far, Thula?

Yes, Mama. I can now.

THE HUNT

Zunga stood with one arm draped over Musa's shoulder, his fingers digging painfully into the muscles of his son's neck. His men stood around their leader waiting for orders. Below them, the herd of elephants stood under the shade of a large Baobab tree.

Zunga pointed off into the distance. "There's the signal. Garai and his men have started the fire." He turned back to his men and nodded to the portable cage sitting on the ground. "You four, take care of the cage."

"What's the cage for, boss?" one of the four men asked.

"We're not just hunting ivory this time," Zunga replied. "We're also after a baby elephant; that one over there with its mother." He pointed to the animal that stood out clearly from the rest of the herd, not only for its smaller size, but also its color. While all the other elephants were varying shades of gray, the baby elephant was a brilliant white.

"White elephants are quite rare," Zunga continued. "They are believed by many to have mystical powers. I don't believe in that mumbo jumbo hogwash, but I sure ain't opposed to capitalizing on it. I already have a buyer for that one."

He felt Musa trying to pull away and tightened his grip. Musa winced but said nothing.

"Okay, everyone to your stations," Zunga ordered. "Wait for my signal."

BIRD WATCHING

Sherlock drove the Jeep out of the compound and careened onto the road heading in the direction of the fire. Suddenly, from the backseat, Ra-Kit shouted, "Stop! Wait a second. Something doesn't feel right."

As Sherlock hauled the Jeep to a skidding stop in a cloud of dust, Zak turned in his seat to glance at the cat. "Really? Now is not the time..."

"Hush!" Ra-Kit cut him off. She looked around, then turned her gaze to the sky.

"But the fire is over there," Zak continued. "I can still see the glow from the flames."

"Who are you talking to?" Nia asked, a confused look on her face.

"He's talking to me," Allie chimed in.

"Don't worry about her," Ra-Kit replied. "She's part of the team, right?"

Zak and Allie stared at each other, then Zak replied, "Yes, she is, but why did you tell us to stop?"

Sherlock turned in his seat and stared straight at Ra-Kit, with a look of awe mixed with confusion on his face. "It's you he's talking to, isn't it?"

Ra-Kit didn't reply, but just kept looking around. For what, Zak had no idea. Sherlock tapped on the steering wheel impatiently.

Finally, Allie spoke up. "What is it? What are we looking for?"

Ra-kit muttered something unrecognizable, then repeated it more loudly. "Nibanna said, 'look for the birds,' but what did he mean?"

"Wait just a minute," Nia interrupted. "Who just said that?" Sherlock pointed to the cat in the backseat, a smile growing on his face.

"Ra-Kit," Zak answered. "I'll explain later." He turned in his seat to look at Ra-Kit. "Who are you talking about?"

But Nia interrupted again. "Did you say, Nibanna? You know him?"

Ra-Kit nodded. "We're old friends, but I don't..." She paused, then pointed with one paw. "There! That's what he meant. I'm sure of it."

Everyone looked in the direction he pointed to see a flock of flamingos flying in a double V formation. "Follow those birds!"

"But that's in the opposite direction from the fire," Zak pointed out.

"Exactly," Ra-Kit replied. "The fire is just a decoy to draw everyone away from the real trouble. Trust me on this point.

Zak stared at Ra-Kit and then to Allie. "Well, she's right more often than she's wrong."

"And she's the one with the magical powers," Allie said. "I think we have to do what she says."

"Magical powers?" Nia said, with a note of awe. "You mean those stories are true?"

Sampson nodded.

"And you can fly?"

Sampson nodded again.

"I must be dreaming," Nia said, as she sat heavily back in her seat.

"Way cool," Sherlock added. "And I thought I had neat friends. Hold on everyone." He threw the Jeep in reverse and turned it around. As he sped away from the fire, the Jeep fishtailed from side to side before he was able to finally straighten it out.

"Careful, Sherlock. Keep it on the road," Nia warned from the backseat.

"No worry. I've got this," Sherlock assured her. "We're off to save the elephants with a magic cat and a flying dog!"

CONFRONTATION

Zunga's men were about to disperse when they heard the rumbling of an approaching vehicle in the distance. "What's that?" Zunga asked, as he turned in the direction of the sound. "Everyone is supposed to be fighting the fire."

"It appears not everyone fell for your little diversion," Musa replied, with a smile of satisfaction.

"Shut up, boy," Zunga said, slapping Musa in the head. "Change of plans for the moment, men. Take cover."

The men scattered away and waited. Less than a minute later, a dirty Jeep pulled up a few yards from where Zunga and Musa stood. Zunga stared at the Jeep for a second before bursting out laughing. "Why, it's just a bunch of kids and their pets out for a morning drive."

He took a couple steps toward the Jeep as it pulled to a stop. "You kids must be lost. What do you think this is, Disneyland? Get out of here before you get hurt." He made a threatening motion toward the Jeep, but stopped when he heard a deep growl from the giant black dog in the backseat.

"Stop what you're doing," Zak yelled as he jumped out, followed closely behind by Allie and Nia. Sherlock slid the gear shift into neutral and applied the parking brake before climbing out as well. "This is an animal sanctuary and you have no business here. Go home."

"Ahh, my new friend, that's Zunga," Sherlock whispered. "I'd tread lightly. He's bad news."

Zunga's men broke from cover and laughed as they slowly circled around the Jeep, their rifles pointing at Zak and the other team members.

"No, it is you who should go home. This land is for anyone who has the strength to take it, and in this instance, that's me and my men." Zunga glanced over to a couple of his men. "If that dog makes so much as a move towards me, shoot him. That goes for the kids as well." He turned back to Zak.

"You look like a smart kid. Clearly you can see you are vastly outnumbered and unarmed. It's time to go home to mommy…now!" With that last comment, he cocked his own rifle and pointed it at Zak.

"Musa, is that you?" Nia said from behind Zak. "What in the world are you doing with these men?"

Musa looked down at his feet but didn't reply, instead taking a step closer to his father.

Zunga glared at his son. "You know this girl?"

Musa nodded.

Zunga smiled. "Well, my sissy of a son is finally growing up. No wonder you're interested in that silly dancing. It's good for attracting the girls, right?"

The look on Musa's face changed from one of embarrassment to anger. "She's right. I have no business here." He turned to walk away.

"Stop right there," Zunga ordered. "What do you think you're doing?"

"This," Musa replied as he grabbed the gun from the man standing next to him. He turned around and pointed it at his father. "She's right. It's time I stood up for what I know is right, and that is that this senseless killing of these majestic animals must stop."

Zunga stepped back, unnerved for a moment by his son pointing a loaded rifle at him, but only for a second, before a wry smile formed on his face. "It's ironic that you would say that while pointing a gun at your father." Seeing that the words had no apparent effect on his son, he tried again. "Listen, son. It's unfortunate that we have to resort to this kind of action just to survive, but that is the truth of it. It's the only way to take care of our village. So, give me that gun and let's get on with what we came here to do."

When Musa didn't move, Zunga let out a deep sigh and waved one arm around to take in the whole scene. "Enough. Look around you, boy. You are still greatly outnumbered. Besides, I've known you all your life. You don't have the guts to use that weapon, especially not against me." He turned to his men. "Let's get on with it…"

But just then Ra-Kit jumped from the back seat over the windshield and onto the hood of the Jeep in a slow graceful arc. The sudden motion drew everyone's attention to her. She sat on the hood and began to clean herself.

"What the…?" Zunga said, momentarily taken aback. "What a scruffy looking cat you've got there, boy," he added, turning in Zak's direction. But Zak wasn't paying any attention to Ra-Kit at that point, but instead looked around him, and smiled as he realized what was about to happen.

"She's not my cat. She belongs to herself..." then, looking around again, added, "...and the rest of the animal world." He pointed upward. Zunga looked up just in time to catch a glob of bird droppings in both eyes, followed a second later by a bombardment from the huge flock of flamingos flying overhead. Their aim was impeccable. Hardly a poacher went untouched, while Zak and his team were unscathed. But the aerial attack was just the first salvo.

As Zunga wiped the bird poop from his face, he looked around through stinging, tear-soaked eyes. Surrounding him and his men was a mass of animals including a pride of lions, a herd of wildebeests and an assortment of jackals, giraffes, rhinos. Interspersed every few yards stood an elephant. Even little Thula stood in the circle, her trunk raised in defiance.

"Nibanna, you came through," Nia spoke up for the first time.

In the distance could be heard the sound of a helicopter approaching. Everyone turned to watch a cloud of dust appear on the horizon as a line of other vehicles approached from the direction where the fire had been.

"I guess Ra-Kit wasn't the only one paying attention to the birds," Allie whispered to Zak.

"Yeah, Dr. Dondi must have seen them as well and radioed a message to David," Zak whispered back.

Musa stepped forward and held out his hand. "It's over, Father." He reached out and took the gun from Zunga's hands. "Order your men to put down their weapons. There need not be any more killing. Not today."

Zunga hesitated for several seconds before finally nodding, his shoulders slumped in defeat.

AFTERMATH

Zak and the rest of the Eco-adventure Team, along with Musa, exited the Constable's office. Sampson wore a collar to which a leash was attached, and even Ra-Kit, who had finally agreed to pretend to be domesticated for a short time, wore a jewel-embossed collar with Allie holding the leash as her owner. They all headed to the cantina where they were to meet Thabiso.

The news wasn't all good. Zunga and his men were all being held for trial in a few weeks, and according to the Constable, it was highly likely they'd be found guilty on several charges of poaching and would face years in prison.

"What was Tokabo doing there?" Allie asked.

"Turns out he was part of Zunga's gang. He told the poachers where to look for the elephants and what we were doing," Zak replied. "I suspect he was also the one who locked us in our rooms.

"At the same time, he was the one who finally told David that the fire was just a diversion from what was really going on. He must have had a change of heart, so David is hoping the judge will be lenient with him. In any case, he'll be spending some time in prison as well."

"I knew there was something fishy about him," Allie said.

"At least the animals are safe at last," Musa said, making an effort to sound positive despite knowing that he and the other villagers were now left to figure out some way to keep from starving.

"Yes, that's true," Zak agreed. "Now we've just got to figure out how to help you and your village."

"Do you have any suggestions?" Musa asked.

Zak shook his head. "Unfortunately, not a one at the moment, but don't give up hope. The team is behind you. We'll figure out something." Still, the day was too gorgeous to not enjoy it, so they all strolled to the restaurant like one happy family.

There they found Thabiso sitting outside at one of the tables, wearing a brightly colored full skirt and several strands of her jewelry, along with bracelets on both arms. She smiled when she saw her son approach.

"Mamma, I want you to meet my new friends. This is Zak and Allie, and Sampson and Ra-Kit." They each nodded, all except Ra-Kit, who simply sat on her haunches and started cleaning herself. "And this is Nia, the girl I told you about."

"It is a pleasure to meet all of you," Thabiso said with a smile. "My son has told me all about your adventures. He told me especially about you, my dear," she continued, nodding towards Nia.

"Oh, Mamma, please," Musa said, blushing.

Nia held out her hand and Thabiso took it. "My, what lovely jewelry," Nia said, as she held Thabiso's hand and gazed at the bracelets.

"Why, thank you," Thabiso replied, obviously pleased by the compliment.

"Making jewelry is my mother's favorite hobby," Musa said. "She just loves making it. She's even gotten several of the other ladies of the village to start."

"Really? How interesting," Nia replied, finally letting go of her hand, but continuing to stare at the necklaces as well.

Musa started to catch his mother up on what he'd learned about his father and the other men of the village. As he did so, Zak noticed that Nia appeared to be preoccupied with something. She suddenly rose from her chair and excused herself. As she walked off, Zak saw her take her phone out of her pocket to make a call, but then Musa asked him a question and he turned his attention back to the conversation. After a few minutes, when Nia had not returned, he leaned over to Allie.

"I'm a little concerned about Nia. Would you mind checking on her? She went in that direction."

Allie frowned. "Well, okay, I suppose so," she replied, clearly not pleased by the request.

"Take Sampson with you," Zak added, handing the leash to her.

Allie nodded, took the leash and walked off in the direction Nia had gone. Zak returned to the conversation.

"I understand that Zunga and his men will need to serve time," Thabiso said, "but what about you, son?"

"No, thanks to my friends here, the Constable was kind," Musa replied. "I have to do twenty hours of community service, but he even said that could be in my village, so I figure I'll be doing more than that anyway."

Thabiso was obviously relieved to learn that her son was not headed to prison along with her husband.

"I just don't know how we're going to make it," Musa continued. "I know the poaching was wrong, but Zunga was right about one thing. It did help provide, not just for our family, but for the rest of the village, too."

Thabiso nodded. She took Musa's hand in her own. "I know, son, but we'll work it out somehow."

"I may be able to help," Nia said, as she and Allie returned arm-in-arm. Both girls were smiling.

"Well, you two seem to have made up," Zak remarked.

"I don't know what you mean," Allie replied defensively. "This girl is remarkable. Just wait until you hear what she's done."

Nia smiled, obviously embarrassed by Allie's words. "Well, I called my dad. Turns out he's been doing some of his own research around the ivory trade. While his company imports a lot of different items, many of them have been works of art carved from ivory. But not any longer. He promised to stop buying or importing ivory, but he said that doing so would create a significant loss of revenue in his business."

"Wow, that's really something," Zak said. "I'm sorry to hear that he's going to take such a loss."

Nia shook her head. "No, that's not it. When he told me, it was a perfect lead-in for me to tell him about your beautiful jewelry," she said, nodding towards Thabiso. "Would you like to sell some of it?"

Thabiso hesitated, taken aback by the question. "Well, sure, I guess, but there's not much of a market for it around here. Like Musa said, several of the other women in my village are making jewelry as well. Some are even surpassing their teacher's efforts."

"Perfect," Nia said, clapping her hands together with excitement. "Because my dad's company wants to buy hundreds of pieces, and if they do well, which I know they will, that could quickly turn into a thousand pieces or more per month."

Thabiso was speechless. Tears welled up in her eyes. Finally, she found her voice again. "I've been praying for months to find a way to help my village without the men having to kill those beautiful elephants. It's been right up there with my prayers to help Musa find a way to continue his dancing. I've even been saving up a little in the hope of one day being able to send him to America to study. There's an African proverb that says, 'When you pray, move your feet', but at the rate I've been able to put aside a little money, Musa will be grown with kids of his own before I'll have enough."

Nia laughed. "Well, no need to keep saving. I made a second call."

"I told you she was amazing," Allie interjected.

"This one was to the dean of my school. It's a school for kids with special gifts in the arts." She turned to Musa. "I had sent him a video I took of you dancing in the square the other day. He would like to offer you a full scholarship to come to America. I also checked with my father and he felt certain we could work it out for you to come as an exchange student and stay with us as long as you like."

Now it was time for Musa to become misty eyed. He hugged his mother first, then Nia. "I'm going to America?"

"If you want," Nia replied.

"I'm going to America!" Musa shouted and began to dance. It may not have been the most graceful dance of his life, but it certainly was the most exuberant. Before long, Zak and the rest of the Eco-adventure Team joined in.

Finally, Nia paused from dancing. "You know, one funny thing I don't understand. When I called my parents, I figured they'd be, I don't know, some combination of angry and worried about where I'd been, but they just seemed thrilled to hear from me."

Zak laughed and pointed to Ra-Kit. "I suspect our little friend there might have had something to do with that. I know she's helped me stay out of trouble with my folks."

"Really?" Nia asked, as she bent over and stared at Ra-Kit. "Did you help keep my parents calm through all this?"

Ra-Kit didn't answer. She simply sat cleaning herself.

The End

Further Resources

I started the Zak Bates eco-adventure series out of my love for the animal world and my desire to make a difference for the many different animals with whom we share this earth. I've learned so much about the special nature of elephants and still have much more to learn. I want to share a few of the resources I used in preparing to write this work of fiction.

Sheldrick Wildlife Trust: Haven for Elephants & Rhinos

https://www.sheldrickwildlifetrust.org/

The David Sheldrick Wildlife Trust, a haven for elephant orphans, rhinos and other animals. Read about our work on elephant conservation, anti-poaching ...

Thula Thula Private Game Reserve

https://thulathula.com/

Thula, best South African safari destination in Zululand with a famous herd of elephants, dedicated to wildlife conservation and protection.
Meet the elephants of Thula Thula (including a glimpse of Thula at the 37 second mark) and the elephant whisperer at:
https://youtu.be/0v9IV8joyxg

Elephant Reintroduction Foundation

worldelephantday.org/about/elephant-reintroduction-foundation

The Elephant Reintroduction Foundation is a charitable non-profit organization based in Thailand. Its goal is to re-introduce captive elephants into their natural habitat. It was founded in 1996, on the initiative of Queen Sirikit of Thailand.

World Elephant Day

worldelephantday.org/

Bringing the world together to help elephants. World Elephant Day in an international annual event on August 12, dedicated to the perservation and protection of the world's elephants.

Animal Poaching Facts | Learn About Endangered Animals
www.unitedforwildlife.org/Endangered
Help Us Help Rhinos, Elephants & Tigers. Learn More and Join Us! Launched In 2014. Follow Our Projects. Illegal Wildlife Trade.

Threats to African Elephants
https://wwf.panda.org/knowledge.../elephants/african_elephants/afelephants_threats/
Despite a ban on the international trade in ivory, African elephants are still being poached in large numbers. Tens of thousands of elephants are being killed every year for their ivory tusks.

Adopt an Elephant Calf
African elephants are family-oriented animals with a complex social structure. There are two types of herds — females with their young and bachelor herds — and lone males.
https://gifts.worldwildlife.org/gift-center/gifts/Species-Adoptions/African-Elephant-Calf.aspx

6 ways to Help Elephants
With the elephant poaching epidemic running rampant, experts fear for the future of these majestic mammals.
https://www.mnn.com/earth-matters/animals/stories/6-ways-to-help-elephants

Dominion Over All

Book 1 of the Zak Bates Eco-adventure series

When the last living magic cat and her flying canine companion show up on your doorstep, you don't expect things to get any stranger!

mybook.to/doa

Endangered

Book 2 of the Zak Bates Eco-adventure series

Protecting the planet: a thankless job and one that has no breaks!

mybook.to/endangered

Porpoise Publishing
Flat Rock, NC 28731
www.lifeonpurpose.com
Library of Congress Cataloging-in-
Publication Data

Ghost Elephant / W. Bradford Swift.
ISBN-10:
1. Young Adult 2. Spirituality 3. Urban
fantasy

Cover design by BetiBup33
Author's photo by B. J. Condrey
Edited by Scott Searle
Printed in USA
First Edition

www.ingramcontent.com/pod-product-compliance
Lightning Source LLC
Chambersburg PA
CBHW030555130626
46552CB00006B/2551